O' WITCHY TOWN OF WHITTLECOMBE

A WONKY INN CHRISTMAS COZY WITCH MYSTERY

JEANNIE WYCHERLEY

O' WITCHY TOWN OF WHITTLECOMBE:

A WONKY INN CHRISTMAS COZY MYSTERY

JEANNIE WYCHERLEY

O' Witchy Town of Whittlecombe:
A Wonky Inn Christmas Cozy Mystery
by

JEANNIE WYCHERLEY

Copyright © 2020 Jeannie Wycherley
Bark at the Moon Books
All rights reserved

Publishers note: This is a work of fiction. All characters, names, places and incidents are either products of the author's imagination or are used fictitiously and for effect or are used with permission. Any other resemblance to actual persons, either living or dead, is entirely coincidental.

No part of this book may be reproduced, distributed or transmitted in any form or by any means, including photocopying, recording, or other electronic or mechanical methods, or by any information storage and retrieval system without the prior written permission of the publisher, except in the case of very brief quotations embodied in critical reviews and certain other non-commercial uses permitted by copyright law.

Sign up for Jeannie's newsletter:
eepurl.com/cN3Q6L

O' Witchy Town of Whittlecombe was edited by Christine L Baker

Cover design by JC Clarke of The Graphics Shed.
Formatting by Tammy
Proofing by Johnny Bon Bon

Please note: This book is set in England in the United Kingdom.
It uses British English spellings and idioms.

CHAPTER ONE

"I'd think about replacing it, if I were you."

The mechanic wiped his greasy hands on a soiled cloth and shrugged. We were standing together under the bonnet of Jed's old van, sheltering from the light drizzle that fell from a mid-afternoon sky, heavy with ominous foreboding. I'd been out running errands, collecting last-minute items for the great Yuletide feast we had planned for this evening when, unfortunately, the van had conked out on the road between Honiton and Whittlecombe.

The mechanic, a ruddy gentleman with fading red hair, a neat beard and bushy eyebrows, had tinkered with my spark plugs and replaced the air filter and a few other things that meant absolutely nothing to me. I'd kind of lost interest after he complained about the third or fourth mechanical gadgety-thingie that was past its prime. I'd retreated into my own little fantasy world, waiting until he finally managed to get the van started again.

I was grateful, but I wanted to be on my way.

Oops. What had he said?

I gave myself a mental shake and focused on him. "Sorry? Replace which part?" He'd caught me out. I felt suddenly guilty for not paying more attention.

He raised his eyebrows as though it were obvious. "All of it."

"Replace the *whole* van?" I asked. He could not be serious. "It's alright, isn't it? I mean ..." I waved my hands around, attempting to encompass symbolically its size and width and general heaviness. "It's ... big. Big things don't break. Not completely. You just fix them."

"Hmmm." The mechanic regarded me with suspicion. "You haven't been driving long, have you?"

I pulled a face. "Not really," I admitted. "But long enough. It's had two MOTs since I"—'commandeered it from a man I turned into a toad' didn't sound quite right—"acquired it." I patted the side of the van. "I thought it was doing alright."

"It has quite a few miles on the clock," the mechanic said. According to the name on his tag, he was a Peter. "And lots of general wear and tear, too.

It's at that age where it's going to start getting expensive to repair. Sometimes it isn't worth it. You might as well cut your losses, hand it in as scrap and find something a little newer."

"That seems rather wasteful to me." I caught my deceased great-grandmother's waspish tone in my own and frowned. *Get back in your box, Gwyn,* I instructed her.

"Well, it's up to you." Peter had the air of an expert who knows he can't talk sense into the vacuous customer he's trying to help. "I'll leave it with you for now. You don't have far to go, do you?"

"Whittlecombe." I glanced down the road as though we could see the village from where we were standing. We couldn't. We couldn't see further than thirty yards. The road took a sharp right after that, the hedges were high, and the day's light was fading.

"Oh, that's right. Eight miles or so. You'll be fine. I'd suggest that at the very least you take it into your local garage and have the starter motor checked out—"

"Alright," I nodded, albeit grudgingly.

"—at your earliest convenience."

"I will. Thank you." Yes, that's exactly what I would do. Replace the wonky bits and nurture the van. Keep it going, until it was the automobile equivalent of the Six Million Dollar Man. More dead than alive. More replaced parts than original.

That kind of appealed to me.

The mechanic gave me one more sardonic look, then released the bonnet prop and dropped the bonnet down over the engine. Exposed to the elements once more, I lifted my face to the drizzle.

"We might have some snow later," I remarked. "Not much. Just a festive sprinkling."

"You think?" Peter peered doubtfully upwards.

"There's ice in that rain," I told him. "Can you feel it?" As darkness started to fall and the temperature varied, there was every chance that those little particles would become snow.

He frowned. "Nah. Too warm for snow."

I ignored that. He was obviously one of those people who can't be told. Their opinions are their entire world view and they're not open to anyone else's.

I smiled instead. "Trust me. I'm a witch. I know what I'm talking about."

"Pfft!" he snorted. "Load of old women's nonsense."

I blinked, slightly insulted. "I beg to differ."

"Witchcraft and fairies. Total poppycock. It's all stories. Although I must say—"

"Must you?" I muttered.

"—folklore is one thing, weatherlore another." He gave an emphatic nod. "I can see there might be something in that, at least."

"I'm not sure what the difference is," I pouted. "It's all part of the same system."

"No, no, no." He had the temerity to wag a finger at me. "Take weatherlore for example, and those countryside almanacs. My old man was into all that sort of claptrap. It's all based on science. It's the kind of stuff our forefathers knew at the dawning of time."

"And foremothers," I corrected him, just for the hell of it really. There's nothing that rankles more than men assuming the world revolves around their sex and theirs alone and always has. The person who originally coined the term '*his*tory' did womenkind a huge disservice.

"Pffft," I continued. "Everything in life is inherently magickal. Anything that *is*, that *exists*, has its own innate magick … if it chooses to utilise it."

"Right." Peter rolled his eyes and edged away, patting his pockets. "Let me get a pen from my cab. I never have one on me, my clients are forever stealing them away from me." He disappeared out of view while I rearranged my scarf around my neck and pulled the hood of my heavy woollen robes up. I didn't mind the drizzle. I found its softness, especially here, so close to the Devon coast, good for the hair and the skin.

I hummed to myself, waiting for him to come back. Despite Peter's general tetchiness, I suppose I was in quite a good mood. My beloved, Horace T Silvanus, known as Silvan, had arrived back following fresh adventures in some forgotten backwater somewhere on the planet. He'd called me earlier once he'd reached Whittle Inn. It sounded as though his journey had taken a few days. He would be tired, but I was ecstatic that he would be at home waiting for me when my errands were complete.

It won't be long, I sang to myself and performed an excited little shimmy in front of the van.

Shakira eat your heart out.

The mechanic cleared his throat. I swivelled round to see him clutching his pen and a pad. He regarded me warily. "Was that a snow dance?" he asked. "Are you calling forth the weather gods?"

"Goddesses," I corrected him. "No, actually. I leave that to my friend, Mara. She's much better at that sort of thing than I am."

"Uh-huh." Peter raised one of his impressively hairy eyebrows.

I folded my arms. "Things must be going well for

her at the moment, otherwise we wouldn't be having this conversation."

"Is that right?" The mechanic didn't sound convinced.

"Yes, she'd have blanketed the countryside in ice and you'd have been driving a snowplough."

"It wouldn't be the first time. I had to do that a few Christmases ago." The mechanic visibly shuddered at the memory.

I understood that shudder. That had been a hairy situation. Christmas had almost been cancelled thanks to Mara the Stormbringer's Snowmageddon.

I nodded in satisfaction. "There you are. That was my friend, Mara."

"Right." He pressed his lips together and held the pad out at arm's length in my direction.

I unfolded my arms and took it from him, scanning the form on top. He'd filled the boxes in for me, enumerating the engine parts he'd replaced, the service charge and the VAT. I whistled when I spotted the total.

"Given that you have a membership, you'll only need to pay for the parts," he explained helpfully.

"Smashing," I said, my good mood threatening to evaporate. "Do I have to pay this now?"

"You can do, if you like. Otherwise, you can send

it via bank transfer. We're all mod cons these days. The information is on the bottom there." He leaned forwards, using his biro as a pointer, trying not to get too close to me, probably fearing my kookiness was contagious.

"I'll do that then," I told him.

"That's fine. If you could sign for me?"

I took the pen and scribbled my signature. He checked it against my membership card, ripped off the top sheet, folded it into quarters and handed it over to me.

"Thank you, Miss Demon," he said and smiled. "Mind how you go, now."

"Daemonne," I muttered. "And thank you, I will." I lifted the hand holding his pen to chest height and wiggled it at him, pretending I was casting a spell. "Hocus pocus," I said.

He shot backwards in alarm, almost tripping over the wheel of Jed's van but managing to grab hold of the side mirror at the last minute and remain upright.

It was mean of me, I admit.

"Sorry, I didn't mean to scare you." I tried hard not to laugh. "But I didn't think you actually believed in witchcraft."

"I don't," he said, but his face betrayed his fear. "It's all mumbo-jumbo."

Impossible man! "Then you have nothing to worry about," I told him and held out his pen. I didn't want to be one of those clients he complained about, you know, the ones who stole his pens.

"Tell you what, you can keep that," he said and beat a hasty retreat to his van. "I'll wait for you to get underway," he called from a safe distance. "If you have any more problems, don't hesitate to give us a quick ring."

"Thanks!" I said, watching as he clambered into his cab.

"Thank you for choosing the Devon Automobile Recovery Service!" he called and slammed the door of his van before I could respond. The tinsel he'd placed around the window jiggled and twinkled with the vibration, getting into the spirit of things even if Peter wasn't.

Giggling, but feeling slightly ashamed of scaring the poor man, I climbed into Jed's van, strapped myself in and turned the key in the ignition. It started up immediately.

"Yay for Yuletide!" I sang with glee. "Let's finish my errands and go home!"

Food, drink, friends and the man I loved were only a few hours away.

What could possibly go wrong?

CHAPTER TWO

I checked my list. Just one more delivery left. I had to drop off a chocolate yule log created by Florence, Whittle Inn's spirit housekeeper, to Mr Kephisto at his bookshop in Abbotts Cromleigh. I stayed for a quick cup of tea and a plate of cinnamon biscuits, of course—it would have been rude not to, after all—and then skipped merrily back to where I'd left the van, admiring the brightly decorated windows of the shops around me. So festive! I squee'd with delight, a small package tucked under my arm. A Yule gift from Mr Kephisto to me.

Happy days!

I couldn't help feeling excited. This would be the first year we would succeed in having a proper Yule time celebration. The inn was full—joyously so, in fact—crammed to the rafters with guests from near and far. Old favourites like Frau Krauss rubbed shoulders with witches from Kappa Sigma Granma, returning for the celebrations while taking the opportunity to spend time with the dearly departed, such as my grandmama, and their own relatives. There were witches and wizards from Salem and Pendle and the New Forest and Glastonbury and Tintagel and Norway and Japan. Some of these guests were scarily dark and mysterious, and I kept my eye on them, but fortunately most of them were cuddly and absent-minded. There were also faeries and goblins and all manner of paranormal beings, just to mix things up a bit.

But best of all, Silvan!

The thought of him waiting at home, no doubt tired, stinking of alpacas, with trench foot because he hadn't taken his boots off for weeks, had me wiggling with happiness. It had been a funny old year, and he'd been coming and going constantly—not always in his habitual form—but now we would make the most of the next few weeks by spending it together.

We intended to have a Yule ceremony in Speckled Wood late that evening to mark the turning of the year. It would be a chance for us to have a bonfire, a jolly old singsong and a bit of dancing.

There would be plenty of tasty treats too, thanks to Florence and Whittle Inn's ghost-chef-in-residence, Monsieur Emietter.

When I'd left the inn a few hours ago, the scent of puddings and pies and roasting meat had made me practically giddy with hunger. Monsieur Emietter, who spoke only French, had issued me with dozens of last-minute ingredient requests that had been translated by my increasingly fraught deceased great-grandmother, Gwyn. I'd driven to a couple of the larger supermarkets in Honiton, stopping along the way to drop off gifts and packages to our friends and neighbours.

Mr Kephisto, the owner of *The Storykeeper* bookshop in Abbott's Cromleigh, had been the final stop. Now, at last, it was time to head home.

I put Mr Kephisto's package on the seat beside me. It looked and felt like a book. I hoped for the newest Stephen King novel because I enjoyed a good literary scare. If I had any time off over the Christmas period—I wasn't expecting a huge amount, but miracles might happen—I fully intended to put my feet up, on Silvan's lap, and read.

I pulled out my mobile and quickly dialled my beloved.

"Hello?" He picked up on the second ring. I heard the smile in his voice.

"Hi!" I said. "Only me."

"Only who?" he joshed. "Is this someone I know?"

"Oh, hush."

"Didn't we speak to each other recently? Like ... an hour ago?"

"More like two, nearly three." I'd insisted he rang me as soon as he reached Whittle Inn because I wanted to know he had arrived safely. I didn't want to leave anything to chance. And besides which, I insisted on taking every possible opportunity to hear his voice. Silvan was a dark witch for hire who went out to remote places in the world and undertook certain missions that other witches didn't want to. That meant that I rarely had the opportunity to speak to him when he was away on a job because he would be deeply undercover or lying low somewhere.

"Really?" He yawned. "I had a nap. Must have been longer than it felt."

"Good. You'll be able to stay up for the party this evening."

"I would never miss a party. I hope you've stocked up on some decent whisky."

"Zephaniah will have that all in hand," I told him. "In a manner of speaking." Zephaniah was a ghost who had lost an arm during the First World War. He'd worked at Whittle Inn before being conscripted and had died at the second battle of Ypres in 1915. Gwyn had later taken it upon herself to visit the battlefield to bring home his ghost orb. He'd worked at the inn with me since I'd arrived a few years ago. He was a lovely young man, softly spoken, and could quite literally turn his one hand to anything.

"What time is it?" Silvan sounded hopeful, probably wanting to crack open a bottle straight away.

"It's eighteen minutes past three," I told him.

"I thought you would have been home by now."

"I had a little adventure with Jed's van," I told him. "It's a bit poorly. We broke down so I had to call out a recovery service." I smiled at the memory of the mechanic scuttling backwards when I aimed his pen at him. "A funny man."

"Did he fiddle under your bonnet?" Silvan asked.

"He certainly put some spark back in my plugs."

Silvan tutted and laughed.

"Listen, I'd better get on," I told him. "I'm only

about ten to fifteen minutes away, so I'll see you in a bit."

"I'll put the kettle on," he promised, but I knew he wouldn't. He'd ask poor overworked Florence to do it.

My very final stop was Whittlecombe Post Office. We had run out of postage stamps back at the inn, having sent out dozens and dozens of both Yule and Christmas cards to people who had stayed with us over the past year or two. We were garnering quite a mailing list. We—or rather my young hotel manager, Charity—would frequently send out newsletters, emails and the occasional text too, but when you're dealing with a variety of extraordinary species and subspecies, it pays to cover all bases. Old-fashioned snail mail had always proved to be a favoured form of communication among our guests and was, therefore, a successful means of marketing.

I parked on double yellow lines—naughty, I know, but I was in a rush—and hopped out of the van. I swept my gaze up and down the road because, although you never see a traffic warden in Whittlecombe, there will always be a first time. The coast seemed clear, and the village looked quiet and festively pretty this afternoon. I lifted my face in appreciation of the abundance of good things in my life. The drizzle was still falling, and I could clearly feel little crystals in the precipitation that landed on my skin.

I pondered whether I should leave the van's engine running while I attended to business inside, but this close to Christmas I was worried how long the queue might be, so I switched off the ignition and trotted into the post office.

I was in luck. There was only one gentleman in front of me at the counter, and one other lady looking at the greetings cards on the spinner by the window. I waited patiently, taking deep happy breaths, inhaling the musty old scent of this place. If you could have bottled it, I'd have worn it as a witchy eau de cologne.

The lady at the spinner left, empty-handed. I stared out of the window, watching her walk away down the street. She turned right and out of sight just as the streetlamps blinked on, glowing a dull, cool orange as they began to warm up.

The gentleman in front of me at the counter

finished his errand and thanked the postmaster. I nodded at him as he passed me. The bell tinkled as he left the shop and I rummaged in my bag to find the cards I needed to send.

Then it was my turn.

"Good afternoon." The postmaster, an older gentleman by the name of Gordon Grey, who ran the post office with his wife, Beatrice, stared expectantly over the top of his wire-rimmed spectacles at me. I couldn't tell from his tone whether he felt it genuinely was a good afternoon or not.

"Good afternoon!" I replied. "Please may I have ... hmmm,"—I hadn't really thought about quantities, but I ought to restock the office—"I'll have sixty first-class stamps and forty-eight second, please."

The postmaster slid an ancient thick leather-bound book out from under the counter. "Would you like the Christmas ones?" he asked, flicking past the first few pages.

I gazed down at the pretty celebratory stamps. The theme this year appeared to be colourful faeries sitting on top of brightly wrapped gifts. I wondered if they'd ever choose witches to front their campaign. They were missing a trick. I'd be happy to pose. I could totally sell the holidays!

The burning question was, did I actually want Christmas stamps *today*? You wouldn't want to be sending those in January and, given that I'd sent most of my cards, I'd be bound to have some left over.

"Ah." I mulled it over for far longer than was really necessary. The huge round clock on the wall behind the postmaster counted down the seconds.

Tick. Tick. Tick. Tick.

Decisions, decisions. "May I have half and half please?"

"Of course," he said, with neither a hint of rancour nor a great deal of goodwill. The Whittlecombe postmaster seemed to have just one expression, and that remained resolutely neutral.

I wondered idly, as I watched him counting out the stamps, what he liked to get up to in his spare time. Was he a closet ballroom dancer? Did he enjoy scuba diving? I studied his balding head as he bent over his stamps, the smattering of freckles and the odd wisps of hair.

I had a feeling he did neither of those things, but I wouldn't have been surprised if he built model railways or collected old coins and medals.

Tick. Tick. Tick. Tick.

"I've had a delivery for Whittle Inn, Ms Daemonne." The postmaster turned to the shelves behind him and quickly located a small package. "I knew you'd be popping in or I'd have had it sent up."

"Thank you." I wondered why it hadn't been delivered in the normal way, but he didn't offer an explanation.

He slid the package and the sheets of stamps over the counter. "Will you be paying with cash or by card?" he asked.

I pulled my purse out of my bag. It felt light; I'd used all my change on parking fees today. That reminded me. I cast a worried eye out at the van. It remained where I'd left it, undisturbed by any sudden appearance of a traffic warden.

Not for the first time today I experienced a rush of guilt. I shouldn't have left it there. And that reminded me of Peter. I wondered how the mechanic was feeling? I hoped he'd recovered from his little scare.

I remembered the look on his face and had a sudden attack of the giggles.

"Ms Daemonne?" The postmaster was waiting for me.

"Oh, yes. Card, please," I said, fishing the trusty oblong of battered and well-used plastic from its pocket and slipping it into the machine. I keyed in my PIN. While I waited for the transaction to complete, I waved the pile of cards I'd extracted from my bag. "And I need to get these in the post, too. Will they go today?"

"Yes, that'll be no problem." The postmaster pointed to a table at the rear of the shop. "Make yourself comfortable over there. Do what you need to do."

From somewhere out the back, a phone began to ring.

"I need to answer this. It's probably the regional office." He started to walk away. "Just leave your cards here on the counter if I haven't returned. I'll add them to the bag in a minute and they'll catch the last post."

"Okay, thanks!" I called after him as he disappeared from view. The phone stopped trilling mid-ring.

"Good afternoon, Whittlecombe Post Office," I heard him say.

I gathered up my stamps, bag, card, receipt, purse and package and slithered to the rear of the shop to dump them on the table there. This was a useful space, conveniently resourced with Sellotape, string, a pair of scissors attached to a chain so they couldn't go walkabout and a number of cheap biros.

The mechanic would have been happy; he could have borrowed a few.

It didn't take me long to stick the stamps onto the envelopes. I felt a pang for the old days when you used to lick the stamps rather than simply peel them off their backing and apply them. The paste had tasted foul, but even so, I was all for the old ways.

I counted the cards. Thirteen of them. Unlucky for some. But not for me, because today was going to be a great day.

Once I'd done with the cards, I pulled the package towards me. It fitted into my hand easily and had been addressed simply to 'the witchy inn', not a person. Probably a Christmas gift for somebody. But who?

'The witchy inn' served to distinguish us from our competitors at The Hay Loft, I supposed.

I turned the package over, hoping for a clue as to the sender, which in turn would help me establish for whom the gift was destined.

A tiny instruction had been sellotaped in place.
Open immediately.
But who *should open it immediately?* I pondered.
Perhaps if I simply removed the outer packaging there would be a further clue inside. A Christmas tag or something similar.

I reached for the scissors and carefully snipped away at the Sellotape until I could peel the layer of packaging back and sneak a peek. There was no further wrapping, just the gift box.

And what a gift box it was!

I slid it out and studied it. Made of some kind of light-coloured wood, it had been hand carved with an intricate design of leaves and flowers. It measured perhaps three inches by three inches and was more than likely a jewellery box of some kind.

Ooh! What if this was a present for me? Perhaps something Silvan had ordered?

If that was the case, then it would be wrong to take a peep inside.

Wouldn't it?

The box sat on my right palm; the fingers on my left hand itched to open the lid.

But ... No!

Just a quick peep.

Don't you remember what happened to Pandora?

I pursed my lips.

Good Alf desperately wanted to put the box back in its wrapping. But the evidence was already there. By peeling opening the outer wrap, I had destroyed any illusion that I hadn't seen the contents.

How would I explain such a breach to Silvan if this was indeed a present from him to me?

On the other hand, Bad Alf wanted to open the box. How could I possibly know what I was dealing with unless I snuck a look?

What would you have done?

I opened the box.

Chapter Three

I stretched the tip of my left index finger out and slowly edged the lid up on its hinges.

I didn't raise it far. There was a mournful sigh. A waft of air. Warm air that blew into my face. The sweet scent of raspberry and cherry candy. I shut my eyes momentarily, cold blue sparks swimming behind the closed lids, then blinked them open again.

The box had fallen from my hand onto the table, the lid open. I hadn't felt the loss of it. Hadn't heard it land.

I righted it. An empty box. Nothing at all inside except a blue velvet padding. Not a jewellery box after all.

Unless something had fallen out of it?

I shuffled through my belongings on the table. There was nothing there that I hadn't been aware of before. I leaned over and checked on the floor. Nothing immediately obvious.

Frowning, I crouched down and peered into the dusty recesses under the nearby shelving. I couldn't see anything. My nose itched and I snuffled.

I would have thought that something as solid as the wooden box would have made some sort of noise as it landed on the table. I hadn't heard anything fall, but perhaps that didn't mean anything? I glanced doubtfully at the pile of Christmas cards. Maybe, because the box had dropped on top of those, I hadn't heard the clunk when it landed.

Or perhaps there hadn't been anything inside in the first place. It could be that the box itself was the gift. I studied it more closely; it was pretty, no doubt about that.

The whole thing was a mystery. I decided my best plan was to head on back to the inn and ask everyone if they knew anything about it. I popped the box, the wrapping, my spare stamps and my purse back into my bag, then shuffled the cards together and walked back to the counter. I waited a few moments. I couldn't hear the postmaster talking, so either he was listening to someone speaking at great length, or the phone call had ended and he was now doing something else. When he didn't reappear,

I placed my cards on the counter as he had suggested.

"Thanks! Bye!" I called out and, when there was no response, I shrugged and made my way outside, pulling the door carefully closed behind me.

The streetlights glowed with a little more warmth now, and the sky was heavy, though not fully dark. The light seemed slightly magickal, I thought. That's the beauty of a winter twilight.

I paused to fumble with my keys. Apart from the slight jangle of them—hidden somewhere at the bottom of my bag, naturally—there wasn't a sound. No birds. Not that the absence of birdsong could be considered unusual at this time of year, when really only the crows and the ravens had anything to say for themselves, but there wasn't even a hint of traffic anywhere, either.

I found my keys and jumped in the van. The starter motor clicked a couple of times, but the engine refused to catch. My heart sank. "Come on," I told it. "Don't make me hate you." At least I could have walked from here. I wouldn't have minded strolling up Whittle Lane to the inn—it wasn't far, after all—I just wanted to get there sooner.

Like right now!

My Sir Galahad, or whatever the dark equivalent of that might be, awaited.

I twisted the keys once more. This time the van coughed into life. "Thank you," I said, smiling at the steering wheel. "You're much too kind."

I checked my mirrors for traffic and, although there was none, I indicated anyway and moved out, ambling up the road at about ten miles per hour. You could never be sure there weren't children, old folks, cats or dogs on this short stretch of the road running through Whittlecombe.

To my left, the lights of Whittle Stores blazed cheerily, the door standing wide open despite the temperature. I couldn't see anyone in the shop, although Rhona appeared to be at the counter. I waved but knew she wouldn't notice me.

On the right was The Hay Loft. I curled my lip as I drove past. Then the coffee shop and the village hall, an A-board outside announcing a Christmas Fayre and Jumble Sale the following day. I made a mental note to call in. No doubt Millicent would be there with a table full of her wonderful pasta sauces, jams and cakes.

And all in aid of a good cause.

So exciting! It was Christmastime in Whittlecombe and now, errands run, I was heading home to my beloved.

I pulled the van into its habitual parking space by the side of the inn, grabbed my bag and jumped out. Glancing up at the sky, it appeared no darker than before, but the crystallised drizzle continued to fall. I held out my arm, watching how the tiniest fragments of ice landed on my sleeve then rapidly melted away.

Snow soon, I nodded to myself. *You wait and see, Peter the Mechanic.*

I tipped my head back and stuck out my tongue, as I'd loved to do as a child, trying to catch the rain or the snow or occasionally the hail, although the latter I'd learned not do again in a hurry. Given the lightness of this wintry shower, there wasn't much satisfaction to be gained in such an activity. I gave it up as a bad job, glad there weren't any windows on the ground floor of the inn on this side.

You could never be sure who'd be watching you.

I made my way around to the front, to enter via the main reception. It had occurred to me that the box might belong to one of the guests, so I intended to ask Archibald, my customer relations and check-in manager, whether he knew anything about it.

Inside, the lights were on, mostly lamps to give mood lighting everywhere, although the stairwells would be properly illuminated. We had one of several large Christmas trees here, and the coloured lights blinked on and off. Archibald was taking a nap at the reception desk, not an unusual occurrence. He was an elderly ghost who needed his rest.

"It's a good job I'm not a guest," I remarked, loud enough to wake him I would have thought, but he didn't move. I tsk-tsk'd but left him where he was. All of my ghosts pulled long shifts, and while it didn't really make any difference to them, seeing as they were already dead, I didn't mind them ghost-napping. You're a long time in the afterlife, after all.

I tucked the box into a hidey-hole under the reception counter, hung my damp robes up in the cloakroom behind the desk and stuck my head inside the main bar. There were quite a few guests sitting around, music was playing on the stereo system—a playlist of chilled jazz Christmas classics by the sound of it—and the fire burned brightly in the grate.

I could see no sign of Zephaniah or Florence, so I assumed they would be in the kitchen. I considered joining them there straight away—Silvan might be hanging out there too, sitting at the kitchen table chatting to Charity and Gwyn—but I decided to nip upstairs first and change into something a little more festive and slinkier.

To kind of set the tone for the rest of the evening, if you know what I mean.

I hummed as I climbed the stairs and walked the length of the corridor on the first floor to my corner of the inn, stepping over an abandoned vacuum cleaner. I found that odd. Where was Florence? The hose was a tripping hazard.

I had a suite on this floor, consisting of the office, my bedroom and bathroom and a small kitchen that I used more as a dumping ground for overspill stuff.

I thought I spied Charity's berry-red hair at the office desk as I went past. "Yoo-hoo," I called without stopping, "I'm back." When she didn't respond, I didn't think anything of it, assuming she was on the phone or up to her neck in lists and spreadsheets.

Pushing open my bedroom door, I stopped in surprise. Silvan was lying on the bed. Not in the bed, but *on* the bed, and not exactly lying, more sort of splayed across the top, one leg dangling over the side.

"Aww," I said quietly. "You *must* have been tired to have conked out like that."

He didn't move. I stood there for a moment,

wondering whether to wake him or let him sleep. It seemed kind of mean to disturb him, so I left him alone and instead dumped my bag on the floor.

By the looks of it, Mr Hoo had been keeping Silvan company. He too snoozed, in his customary place, perched on the bedstead. I reached out and stroked his soft head. He didn't move.

Didn't even twitch.

"Everyone is so tired today," I said, not trying to keep my voice down anymore. I was beginning to feel a little peeved that nobody was pleased to see me. I'd had a hard day playing both Mother and Father Christmas, with a bit of goddess-of-the-Yule for good measure, and nobody seemed to care.

I pulled off my robes and tutted, chucked them on the floor and made a beeline for the bathroom. I might as well have a bubble bath and make myself look and smell gorgeous.

Or attempt to.

"Florence?" I called, gagging for a cuppa.

I turned the tap and waited for the water to run warm, crossing my fingers the boiler wasn't on the blink again.

"Florence?" I pushed the plug into the hole and reached for my current favourite bubble bath, strawberry and thyme. Not particularly seasonal, but I had no doubt that someone—probably Millicent—would gift me something slightly more festive over the next few days.

"Florence?" The third time I called her name, I frowned.

Of course, she might have been tied up with a guest, I appreciated that, but she tended to apparate in and out so quickly, even if just to tell me she would be back shortly, that her non-appearance struck me as peculiar.

I turned off the tap, allowing the silence to fill the room. I couldn't hear the timbers of the old inn responding to the movements of my guests. There were no doors slamming, no excited voices, no laughter.

I dried my hands and stepped back into the bedroom, staring down at the sprawled form of my lover.

"Silvan?" I queried, edging alongside him. Perhaps he had been drinking. I sniffed gently. No scent of whisky, his favourite tipple, just the faded musky fragrance of patchouli and Arabian rose.

I drew back. For the first time, I noticed that he only had one boot on; the other lay on the floor where he'd dropped it. He'd obviously been sitting on the bed taking them off when he had fallen asleep.

Weird.

I reached down to caress his face, half afraid that he would be cold to the touch. My fingers hovered in the air, the muscle memory of other corpses I had touched, however reluctantly, stored in my fingertips.

"No!" I said, as though by vocalising such a stark refusal it would banish any chance that someone I loved might have suffered the same fate.

With brash confidence I smoothed Silvan's forehead, flicking the hair away where it had fallen over his eye. His skin was cool but not cold. I reached for his shoulder and shook him gently. "Silvan?" I whispered. He didn't stir. His eyes didn't even flicker. I shook him harder. "Silvan?" I couldn't help the note of alarm in my rising voice. "Wake up!"

His head rolled to the side, exposing his throat. Instinctively, I checked for a pulse. He had one. Slow and strong.

I frowned and stepped back, looked from him to my owl.

"Mr Hoo?" I asked.

He slept on, his huge eyes hidden, his adorable chin on his feathery chest.

"Hello?" I said loudly, but neither of my favourite boys responded.

Shaking my head, I crouched down and unlaced Silvan's remaining boot, dropping it on the floor beside its friend, then slid his leg onto the bed and straightened him up. He was heavier than me and it took quite a lot of effort on my part, but not once did he moan or groan about my rough treatment of him. He remained as limp as a dishrag.

Mr Hoo produced the tiniest snoring noise, cute as a button. I gently buried my fingers in his thick wad of feathers. He was warm. Alive. But he didn't stir at my intrusion.

Flummoxed, I glanced around the room. I'd heard of carbon monoxide poisoning and wondered for a moment whether that's what I was dealing with here. I'd had intermittent boiler issues for the past two years. Wasn't carbon monoxide poisoning the result of a faulty boiler or heating system?

I swallowed.

But then again, Silvan didn't have the characteristic pink colour associated with carbon monoxide poisoning ... and so far, I felt absolutely fine. Not even slightly light-headed. Nonetheless, unwilling to take the risk, I padded over to the window and flung it open, the instant rush of cold air reminding me I was only partially clothed.

I gathered up my robes, still warm from my body heat, and pulled them on once more.

"You guys stay here," I told the sleeping pair. "I'll go and—" I didn't really know what to go and do. Find Florence? Consult Gwyn? Ask Charity for help?

Charity was closest. Just next door.

"I'll be back," I said.

Alf the terminator.

Charity had started growing her hair out after our Witchywood experience. I'd put that down in part to her wanting a more versatile head of hair to style as she saw fit. In honour of the winter season and our planned festivities, she had died her short, chin-length bob a bright berry red. I loved it, but we now clashed, given that my wild and untamed mop was naturally a kind of flame orange.

I'd spotted the flash of her hair as I'd swanned past the office only five minutes before, so I anticipated her still being at the desk in front of the computer. I burst into the room through the open door.

"Charity?" I started. "Have you any idea—"

I lurched to a stop.

Charity was slumped in the seat, her shoulders rounded, her chin on her chest.

"Charity?" I repeated. "Hello?"

No response.

I gulped. "This isn't funny."

But please let them all be playing a trick on me. Ha ha! Very funny! Time to move on ...

I moved towards her, placed my hand gently on her upper arm and gave her a little shake. Her head fell further forwards and I jumped out of my skin. "By all that's green!"

Clutching a hand to my heart, I knelt beside her so that I could look up into her face. Her eyes were closed, her muscles relaxed. Her chest rose and fell.

Asleep. That's all!

"Okay ..." I drew in a shaky breath, once more looking about me as though the room would yield some sort of clue. It didn't. Everything appeared normal. The fire in the grate burned as it always did. There was a ring of screwed-up paper balls around the wastepaper basket. Beyond the window, the world burned with that peculiar late afternoon light

I'd noticed before. The world held its breath, waiting for night to fall.

"Gwyn?" I called. She didn't appear at once but, unlike Florence, that was nothing unusual. Gwyn was a law unto herself. She did what she wanted, when she wanted.

I tipped my head to listen. The timbers of the inn didn't so much as creak.

"Gwyn?" I knew she wasn't coming.

A shiver of unease ran down my back. "Alrighty, then," I said quietly. Hearing the sound of my own voice lifted my confidence somewhat. I marched out of the room and took the back stairs. Halfway down I stopped, listening to the sound of Christmas jazz as it drifted from the bar. But that was the only sound I could hear. Turning right at the bottom of the stairs, I made my way along the passage to the kitchen.

I pushed open the kitchen door, to be greeted by the scents of roasting meats and sausages wrapped in bacon, figgy pudding and berry compotes. A huge cauldron containing Monsieur Emietter's rich winter broth sizzled on top of the stove. I eyed my rotund French chef asleep in his rocking chair next to the fire. His moustache twitched as though his breath—in and out—caught at it. This was impossible, of course. Monsieur Emietter, as a ghost, was incapable of breathing.

"Monsieur?" I called, and when he didn't reply, I tip-toed past him to examine the evening's fare. I lifted the lid of the iron cauldron and inhaled, my stomach rumbling. The liquid bubbled and I reached to turn it down, wondering whether to turn it off altogether.

"Florence?" She would know.

But she still didn't apparate.

My heart sank.

I gave the soup a stir and replaced the lid, then retraced my steps to the back passage, past the stairs and The Snug and The Hug. Both rooms were empty, but fires burned in the grates. Florence had been busy. So where was she?

I pushed open the door to the bar and stood stock still, taking in the scene in front of me. The smooth sound of a jazzed-up version of *O' Little Town of Bethlehem* rang out. The room was decorated for Christmas, of course. We had painstakingly festooned an enormous Christmas tree with a range of colourful baubles. Charity had wanted a classy look and tried to insist on a matching colour theme for the tinsel and balls, but I loved rainbow colours and the sheer diverse collection of Christmas tat I'd found in a chest in the attic before my first eventful Christmas at my wonky inn a few years before. There'd been decorations in that chest that had been carved from wood and hand painted that probably dated back well over a hundred years. Now those, along with glass baubles, tin baubles, brittle plastic figures from the sixties, crocheted stars and felted animals had been put to good use. I'd personally ensured that dozens and dozens of eclectic and eccentric items had made it onto one of the three trees that graced the ground floor of Whittle Inn.

A jolly spectacle.

Except ... it wasn't.

As I stood there, the music came to an end. I swivelled my head. We kept the stereo behind the bar's counter. Only now did I notice Zephaniah, slumped in the corner, his head lolling on his shoulders. He'd been in the process of washing something up. Water still cascaded into the sink. I slid in behind the counter and twisted the tap off, then turned back to the bar, the corners of my mouth quivering.

Twenty or so of my guests, who had been enjoying a high tea prepared by Florence or a sneaky afternoon gin and tonic, were sprawled in their seats, eyes closed, mouths slack, one or two dribbling. I moved out from behind the bar and walked among them, checking for any signs ... not of life ... but of death.

To my relief, everybody seemed fine. They were just ... asleep.

I massaged my forehead. What should I do?

"Gwyn?" I tried once more to reach my great-grandmother. "Florence? Anybody?"

When nobody came, I walked back behind the bar, picked up the huge receiver of the ancient Bakelite phone and put it to my ear. My finger poised over the dial, but when I didn't get a tone, I tapped the cradle instead. "Hello?" I tried, as though somewhere, somehow, there was an operator manning the exchange and I, in a clipped wartime accent, would say, 'Whittlecombe 248 requests assistance. Urgently.'

And how would this mythical operator respond?

'On its way, Whittlecombe 248. Do keep calm. Carry on.'

"Pip pip," I said into the dead air beyond the receiver and carefully replaced it.

My mobile phone! Of course!

I'd left it in my bag at reception. I hurried through the bar area and out into the lobby, where Archibald was still taking what I'd assumed was a cat nap. Fumbling in the bag, among sheets of stamps, stray sweets, tissues, receipts, a rather old apple and numerous other entirely-essential-but-useless bits and bobs that weigh down any woman's life, I sought it out. Eventually I found it. I thumbed the screen.

Who you gonna call?

Millicent Ballicott. My best friend and fellow witch who lived down in the village. She was older than me and more experienced. She would know what to do. But even as I searched for her number, I realised that the phone had no signal.

"What is going on here?" And now I sounded properly irked.

I switched the phone off and powered it up again. While I was waiting for it to do its thing, I stepped through the front door, staring up at the sky, the light icy drizzle still falling, sparkling in the light that burned from the windows. My phone binged and bonged, but when it had finally settled down, there was still no signal.

"I really don't understand," I grumbled, holding the device above my head and twisting this way and that. If anybody had been watching they would have assumed I was performing some kind of archaic and celebratory Yule dance. It didn't make any difference which way I contorted myself, I still didn't increase the number of bars on the display from zero.

I scowled. "Typical! Why can I never get a signal when I really need one?"

I stomped back inside, peeked hopefully into the bar where everyone still slept, then returned to the reception desk and picked up the phone there. This was a more modern one. Digital. The screen glowed, but when I held the handset to my ear, there was still no ringtone.

It was beyond a joke now.

Someone, somewhere, *had* to be awake. They had to be!

I took the main stairs up to the first floor and tapped on the first guest room. When there was no answer, I tried the door. Unlocked. Inside I found a witch asleep in an armchair, her cat dozing at her feet. I bent to pet the cat, but it didn't move a whisker.

I left them in peace and moved out to the corridor once more. I instinctively knew I could enter every guest room but the result would be the same. I decided to try one more room. Frau Krauss had, as usual, occupied her preferred suite on the second floor. This was a small room, decorated sparsely in forest green and with mute white walls, but it was a room with a turret that looked out over Speckled Wood in the near distance. I trotted up the stairs, knocked impatiently on her door and turned the handle. The room was empty. Frau Krauss, a green witch, was evidently out foraging or communing with small mammals somewhere.

I walked to the window and gazed out, umming and ahhing. If Frau Krauss was in Speckled Wood, perhaps she would have escaped whatever had happened here.

And Finbarr too! As annoying as the little Irish witch was—and his irritating pixies—it would be good to have some company as I navigated whatever was going on here in my wonky inn.

Should I go out and search for either of them? I wasn't sure that made sense. They could be anywhere. Finbarr would be back for dinner soon, surely? And Frau Krauss too. She wouldn't want to miss the Yule festivities.

There was only one thing for it. I would have to run back down to the village and drag Millicent back up here. I'd let her take a look and heed her advice.

I trusted her wisdom.

CHAPTER FOUR

I wrapped up against the chill and headed back out into the twilight. It occurred to me to take the van back into the village, but that seemed a little lazy. If I walked quickly, I could be at Millie's in five minutes. I didn't want to spend too long away from the inn, not least because I'd left the oven on and I was worried that Frau Krauss and Finbarr would return and be overcome by whatever was causing the sleeping malaise.

The sleety-drizzle covered my robes as I briskly walked along the lane towards Whittlecombe. My breath sounded loud in the quiet of the early evening, partly from my exertion, partly with nerves. I couldn't hear the slightest rumble of traffic, and it struck me yet again that this was quite unusual.

Before long, I spotted the door to Hedge Cottage. I sped up, longing to hear a familiar voice. Warm light glowed from the front window. She was home! Hooray.

I tapped on the door. Normally this would have been a cue for all hell to erupt. Millicent had two dogs, a hairy lurcher named Jasper and a Yorkshire terrier she'd inherited, named Sunny. Between the pair of them, they could effectively warn off a burglar or trespasser within two hundred yards.

But today ... nothing. Not a yap, not a growl, not even a sneeze.

My heart skipped a beat.

I knocked a little harder. "Please be in," I said, but no-one came.

I turned the door handle and let myself in. "Helloooo?" I called. Nothing furry rushed towards me, intent on wagging me to death or giving me a good face wash. Millicent didn't greet me in her usual cheery tone. In fact, she didn't greet me at all. I stepped out of the narrow hallway and into Millicent's living room. The lamps had been turned on to ward off the gloom, and her wood burner glowed with heat. A freshly woven garland, crafted from pine branches, holly and ivy and decorated with silver bells and red berries had been hung along the mantelpiece. The overall effect was cosy.

Millicent was sitting in her usual place on the

sofa, her head lolling back against the seat. The knitting in her lap was a brightly coloured, half-finished Christmas jumper, abandoned in mid-row. My heart gave a now-familiar hop of fear, but as I approached, I could see the rise and fall of her chest.

Asleep.

I knew it would do no good, but I tried anyway.

"Mills?" I whispered, shaking her shoulder gently. Her head rolled.

"Millicent?" I asked, more loudly this time. She sighed softly but didn't open her eyes.

I stared down at her. She seemed peaceful. I wondered if any of these Whittlecombe sleepers were dreaming? And if so, what about?

I hoped the dreams were pleasant ones.

I cast around, wondering what to do, but in the end there was nothing that could be done. I grabbed a cushion from the armchair and slipped it behind my friend's head, trying to make her comfortable. Then I gently prised her knitting from her hands—some ghastly orange reindeer was trying to take shape there by the look of it—and covered her up with a patchwork blanket she kept neatly folded on the back of the sofa. I didn't want her to get cold after all. The night would soon be upon us ...

I paused mid-thought.

It occurred to me that I'd been thinking that same thought for some time. *It will soon be dark. It will soon be night-time.* And yet, the light outside hadn't changed. It had been twilight for what felt like hours.

Frowning, I made my way to the front door and pulled it open, staring upwards. I hadn't been imagining it. It should have been full dark by now, but instead, the sky remained unchanged, a strange kind of grey-purple hue with the sort of odd glow that gives you a bit of a headache.

The gloaming.

I retreated inside once more and glanced at the carriage clock that Millicent kept on her mantelpiece. Three fifty-eight. Not quite four o'clock. That simply wasn't possible. I crept closer to the fire, the heat warming my knees, and bent down to listen to the clock. It ticked contentedly enough, but the second hand didn't move.

"Huh?" I tapped the glass face gently, flicking it with a fingernail. That didn't improve matters. The clock continued to tick. The second hand remained resolutely in place.

"Maybe it's been broken for a while," I said, but I could hear the doubt in my own voice.

From the direction of Millicent's small kitchen

came the pitiful sound of a whimper. The dogs! I bounded the few steps to the door—which was already open—and popped my head around. Jasper, Millicent's big hairy lurcher, and Sunny, the tiny Yorkie she'd rescued, both stared up at me through round, black eyes. Sunny shook noticeably, wedged tightly against Jasper's front legs, but Jasper appeared more stoic than afraid.

"Hey, guys!" I cooed, "It's me, Alf! You know me." I knelt down and held out a hand, rubbing my fingers, trying to coax them over. "Come on. Come and see me."

Neither of them moved.

"Did something scare you?" I asked, as though either of them could answer me. "What was it? Do you know what it was?" Right at that moment I would have given my right arm to speak dog, but I didn't.

"Come on," I repeated. "It's alright."

Jasper nudged Sunny with his nose. She cried out.

"Awww," I said. "Come on, baby." I held my hand further out, and this time Sunny sniffed the air between us before taking a tentative step towards me.

"Good girl, that's the way." I kept on encouraging her until finally she was close enough that I could have grabbed her collar, had I wanted to. I didn't, of course. I just let her do her own thing, sniffing nervily around me until I could stroke her head. Jasper followed her, less reticent, and when Sunny had had enough fuss—if such a thing is ever possible—he lay his head on my knee and stared up at me with the most soulful of expressions.

"I know," I told him. "I haven't a clue what's going on either." I stroked his great furry head. "I am so pleased to see you chaps though, you have no idea. You're the first living—I mean, awake—people, folks, dogs, beings, whatever, I've seen in what feels like a lifetime."

I noted the clock on Millicent's oven, glowing green. Three fifty-eight.

"But is actually no time at all," I finished softly.

I stood and moved backwards into the living room, the dogs sticking to me like velcro. I scrutinised the contents of the room, trying to spot anything out of place or anything that shouldn't have been there. But just as I'd found at the inn, everything seemed normal.

With the exception that Millicent was asleep, and I couldn't wake her up.

Jasper trotted towards Millicent and placed a

paw on her thigh. When she didn't respond, he looked and me and whined.

I grimaced. "I don't know what to do or how to wake them," I told him. "I've an inn full of sleeping people." I reconsidered that. "And an owl. And a cat. And ghosts too. It's mighty peculiar."

He cocked his head, taking in every word.

"I think I'd better head back up there," I told Jasper. "If I can figure this out, I'll come back and—"

I didn't get any further. He barked sharply and ran to the front door. Sunny's head swivelled, watching him, then, when it became apparent what he was doing, she ran after him. The pair of them were barring my way.

"Come on, guys," I begged. "I need to get back. I promise—"

"Woof!" Jasper had a deep bark. My ears vibrated in the titchy hallway.

"By all that's green," I grumbled.

I cast one last yearning glance at Millicent, then turned reluctantly to the dogs. "I suppose I could take you both with me."

"Woof!" This seemed to meet with Jasper's approval.

"Just temporarily, so that you're safe. Think of it as an extra walkies," I told him. "Although I'll be glad of the company if I'm honest. It's a bit unnerving being the last witch standing."

I reached up to a hook behind the door where Millicent kept her grubby old walking jacket. I found the dogs' leads behind it and clipped them on. Sunny was still shaking but she seemed keen to get out of the house. The second I opened the front door, the pair of them yanked me out into the gloom and along the path. At the pavement I pulled them to a stop, checking up and down Whittle Lane for any sign of life.

No cars, no people, no sound. Some of the cottages had their curtains open or blinds pulled up and light spilled out. I could spot Christmas trees winking away behind some windows, but in other places, the houses remained dark as though the residents were still at work. I puffed out a couple of hard breaths, observing the steam. Still not cold enough for snow, but getting there.

"I wonder …" I said, and pulled the dogs to my right, heading for Whittle Stores.

If I'd been hoping to find some life in any of the village shops I was quickly divested of that notion.

When I'd driven past Whittle Stores earlier—and how long had that been? At least an hour ago—I'd imagined I'd seen Rhona at the counter serving. But here she was, slumped over that same counter. Stan had collapsed in the door to the stockroom, his head propped up by the doorframe, a cabbage in his lap. One of their customers was splayed on the floor, snoring loudly, surrounded by mushrooms.

When I say surrounded by mushrooms, I don't mean that the woods had encroached on Whittlecombe and reasserted its primary right to exist anywhere and everywhere, thereby coating the shop floor with forest detritus. No, no. I mean, of course, that the customer had been purchasing mushrooms for her supper and, at the moment she had fallen asleep, she had sunk to the floor and released her grip on her basket. As a result, the mushrooms had rolled everywhere.

By force of habit, I stooped and began collecting them together. I realised it seemed a strangely banal thing to do, surrounded as I was by people sleeping where they shouldn't have been sleeping. Nonetheless, I popped as many mushrooms as I could find into the cardboard basket and returned it to its rightful place on the shelf between the Brussel sprouts and some white carrots that were on offer.

Ewww. White carrots.

The shop door had been left open, and the whole place was as cold as a refrigerator. I wondered whether Stan and Rhona would freeze to death before I found out the cause of this strange sleeping illness. And that put me in mind of anyone else in Whittlecombe who had been out and about. What about Frau Krauss and Finbarr in Speckled Wood, for example?

Time was pressing—if not passing—and I had to get to the bottom of this.

At the door where I'd left him and Sunny, Jasper growled. I looked up, hoping to see some other sign of life—perhaps Millicent had come back to life and come in search of her dogs, but no. My dogs had been joined by another two. A large, slightly overweight golden Labrador that I recognised as belonging to one of Millicent's neighbours, and an exceedingly pretty sleek grey whippet, so slender she could have disappeared behind a lamppost.

"Oh, hello!" I said, my voice sounding eerily loud in the silence. I lowered it. "Where have you two come from? Any owners with you?" I moved towards them, peering out into the grey light. Nobody to be seen. It had been too much to hope for.

I sighed.

The golden Labrador slipped past me. I made a grab for him, but he was too quick. He darted straight for the pet food shelves and picked up a packet of dog biscuits.

"Hey!" I chastised him and quickly pulled them out of his grip. He dropped to a neat sit and lifted a paw.

"Very cute," I told him, putting the biscuits back on the shelf, "but you shouldn't be in here."

I was about to shoo him out when I realised that if I intended to take Sunny and Jasper back to Whittle Inn, I would need some dog food. How much depended on how long I expected all this to go on for, of course.

Stepping carefully over Stan, I slid behind the counter and helped myself to one of the hessian bags-for-life that Rhona kept there. I filled it with cans of dog food and biscuit mix and, as an extra measure, dropped in a few treats.

The golden Labrador whined.

"They're not for you," I told him. "You have a home."

He whined again.

"Don't you?"

He looked sad.

"Oh." I stared out at the step where the other

dogs had congregated, and now by the look of it, there was a pug waiting for me too. The whippet shook as though she were cold. Where had she come from? I couldn't leave her out in this weather.

"Alright!" I grabbed another bag-for-life and went through the same process of filling it up again, until I had half-emptied poor Rhona's shelves. I fished around for my purse and did a quick calculation of how much I probably owed, sucking my teeth at the expense. "You guys aren't cheap," I grumbled, standing in front of the till and slipping the notes through the tiny gap in the cash drawer. I came back round to the shop side and lifted the bags.

"Blimey." The contents of these bags would ensure I had a decent workout just walking up the road to the inn. I stepped outside amongst the dogs—they'd now been joined by some kind of fluffy white Jack Russell type thingummy hybrid—and set the bags down on the pavement so that I could unclip Sunny and Jasper. There was no way I'd be able to hold on to the dogs and carry my shopping. Stuffing their leads into the shopping bags, I turned and firmly closed the shop door. A two-foot-high neon snowman twinkled at me from the other side of the glass.

How delightfully cheery.

I turned back to my furry charges. "Right, you lot. I'm going to trust you guys to walk with me like civilised beings," I informed them. "The slightest hint of trouble and you'll either spend all night in the shed or"—I considered my options—"I'll turn you into cats."

There was a collective whine.

"Good!" Having clarified the situation for them all, I clucked like a mother hen. "Let's go!"

We didn't get very far.

I'd only made it to the post office before I had to drop the bags and rest my arms. The door was closed but the light was on inside.

"Wait here," I instructed the dogs.

The golden Labrador began sniffing at the hessian bag. "Ah-ah-ah!" I told him and he backed off, lending me a little stink eye.

I pushed the door open, hearing the familiar jangle, breathing in the musty scent. "Hello?" I called.

There was no response.

Tick, tick, tick.

I stepped inside. There on the counter, exactly

where I'd left it, was my pile of Christmas cards. Evidently, the postmaster had not returned to the shopfront, and nobody had visited after I'd left the premises.

"Hello?" I tried again, more softly. Moving to the counter, I craned my head to see through to the back. I thought I could see the grey material of the postmaster's trousers, but I wasn't entirely sure.

Swallowing, uncertain of the legality of being on the wrong side of the post office counter, I pulled up the counter flap, pushed open the latched door and squeezed through. "Hi? Anyone there?"

The postmaster was sitting on a stool, his face planted on his desk. He'd been on the phone. The receiver lay beside him. I gingerly reached for it and held it to my ear. The line buzzed with energy as I listened. I had the impression that someone was on the other end, although that made no sense. "Hello?" I said. "Can you hear me?"

The clock ticked.

There was no reply.

I waited, giving them every opportunity to say something, but, given the amount of time that had elapsed since everyone went to sleep and now, it seemed unfeasible that someone would hang around for that length of time.

And that got me thinking.

The clock on the wall behind the counter, just like Millicent's, continued to tick, and yet it had stopped at three fifty-eight.

It must have been around that time that I'd been in here.

I left the postmaster where he was and slipped back into the post office itself. What had I been doing? I'd been sitting at the table at the rear and experienced that funny moment. Had that been three fifty-eight? Was all this something to do with me or just a coincidence? If everyone else in Whittlecombe was asleep, why wasn't I?

I moved over to the table, remembering how I'd opened the box and lost all sense of where I was. Then I'd discarded the wrappings and gone about my business. There hadn't been anything in the box and I'd gathered up my rubbish and chucked it into the wastepaper basket under the table.

I crouched down and pulled the wastepaper basket towards me. My own crumpled-up offerings lay on the top. I hoiked them out and examined the torn brown paper. The 'witchy inn' address was obvious, but there was no return or forwarding address. I dug around a little more in the wastepaper basket, just in case there had been a note that I'd overlooked, but there wasn't anything apparent. Then I knelt down and had a quick scan of the floor again.

Nothing I'd missed the first time.

Crumpling the rubbish up once more, I stuffed it inside the pocket of my robes.

"It's a mystery," I said aloud, and went outside to rescue my shopping before the golden Labrador gave in to temptation. I led my growing entourage of canine companions up the lane towards my wonky inn.

CHAPTER FIVE

All the timepieces in the inn still said three fifty-eight.

My body clock, on the other hand, told me it was nearer eight. I should have been completing the evening dinner service, joking with Charity and making ready for our Yuletide festivities, excited for the night ahead. Instead, I felt exhausted and dejected, and my arms were twice as long as they had been before I'd purchased all the dog food.

I checked on Silvan and Charity upstairs, but both were still slumbering. Nothing had changed.

In despair, I realised that I needed to talk to somebody with more experience of dealing with oddities and absurdities than me. I rooted around in my wardrobe until I located the box that contained my orb, then marched back downstairs. A pack of hungry dogs eyed me longingly.

There were nine of them now: Jasper, Sunny, the golden Labrador, the sleek, velvety whippet, the pug, the fluffy Jack Russell type thingummy hybrid, something that looked like a yeti that had been waiting for me when I stepped out of the post office, and a pair of border collies from a nearby farm who had joined us as we walked up the drive. I couldn't stand their pitiful looks for much longer, so I fed them all with the food I'd bought at Whittle Stores and helped myself to a bowl of Monsieur Emietter's good vegetable broth that had been simmering on the stove for hours. The lovely aromas wafting through the inn had rekindled my appetite. I'd checked on the roasting meat, and curiously, while the ovens were both still on and giving out heat, nothing appeared to be burning.

It had to be magick.

The broth gave me a boost of much-needed energy, but I still felt somewhat downhearted. In definite need of some sage advice, I made myself a cup of tea and pulled my orb towards me, rubbing the dust from the surface with its velvet covering.

The orb sparkled and bubbled. For a moment I had the sinking feeling that this, like the phones in the house, wouldn't work either, but I needn't have feared. After a slight delay, Wizard Shadowmender popped up and smiled.

"Alfhild," he boomed, his snowy moustache twitching. "Yuletide greetings to you! You just caught me. I'm on my way to the Grand Yule Ball at the Ministry." He meant the Ministry of Witches. He pulled his orb away from himself so that I could take in his magnificent scarlet and gold ceremonial robes.

"You look splendid!" I told him. "You've even brushed your hair and beard." I'd never seen him look so perfectly coiffed.

"Cheeky," he responded, but his eyes twinkled. "What can I do for you on this auspicious evening, Alf?"

"I'm sorry to bother you. Truly," I said. "It's just ..." I cast around for the word to explain, "... everyone here is asleep. As though they've been hexed."

"Everyone at Whittle Inn is asleep?" he repeated, his brow crinkling.

"Everyone at the inn *and* in the village." I picked up the orb and swivelled it around so that he could see Monsieur Emietter asleep in his chair by the range. "Even the ghosts."

"You've tried to wake them up?"

I raised an eyebrow.

"Well of course you have." Wizard Shadowmender chuckled softly. "What about magick?"

Now, I'm not and never have been the world's best spellcaster. It had crossed my mind to use a little magick, a wake-up incantation of some kind, but with any spell, you have to know what you're working with. You can never be quite sure that magick cast by someone else hasn't been booby-trapped in some way. In all honesty, I hadn't been confident enough to try anything out.

I shook my head in response to his question. "I thought about it," I admitted, "but I daren't. I don't want to make things any worse."

"Hmm." Wizard Shadowmender pursed his lips. I watched him retreat inside his own head, considering what I'd told him. Eventually he looked back at me. "When did this happen? Did you see anything?"

I shrugged. "I'm guessing it happened at three fifty-eight. All of the clocks in the village stopped at that time. And I didn't *see* anything—" I hesitated.

"But?"

"But I may have *felt* something."

"Tell me."

"I was in the post office, and the postmaster had given me a little parcel that for some reason had arrived there and not been delivered directly to the inn. It didn't have a name on it so I opened it myself." I held up the intricately carved box.

He bobbed closer to the glass his end so that all I could see was one eye and his nose. "Can you hold it closer?"

I brought it up against the crystal orb so that he could get a better view of it.

"That's very beautiful," he said. "Was there anything in it?"

"Not a thing. I opened it up, felt a little light-headed for a moment, but after that I was fine."

"And when did you first notice everyone else was asleep?"

"Not long after that. I arrived back at the inn and rushed upstairs to see Silvan." My voice caught. "I haven't seen him for a while and I was so excited, but he was sound asleep on the bed. So sound that I couldn't wake him. Or Mr Hoo," I remembered. "And then I found Charity, and so it went on."

"And everyone in the village?"

"I went down to Millicent's house and she was out for the count too. And people in the shop. In fact, absolutely everyone as far as I can tell. I'm the only one left awake."

Beneath the table, lying on my feet and doing a good job of warming them, Jasper gave a little bark.

"The only *person* left awake," I corrected myself. "It seems that dogs have been excluded from the sleepyhead club."

"Now *that* is intriguing," Wizard Shadowmender nodded. "Our first clue!"

"Is it?" I couldn't quite see the link myself.

"It does sound exceedingly like a Somnus hex, or the Sleeping Beauty curse as we often call it."

"A Somnus hex," I repeated. I'd never heard of it, but I guessed its alternative name told me everything I needed to know about it. "But why have I been spared?" Jasper shifted position, reminding me I was not the be-all and end-all in this strange universe. "And the dogs? Why didn't we all fall asleep too?"

Wizard Shadowmender rubbed his beard. "I'm not really sure of the answer to that," he replied.

I hadn't been expecting to hear such a confession. One always assumes that a wizard as powerful as Shadowmender would know everything. My face must have fallen because he smiled at me. "Now don't look like that, Alfhild. *I* might not know, but I do have a wizard acquaintance who may be able to help you. You'll have to come to London though."

"London?" If I sounded horrified, it was only because I was. The inn was full of the delicious scents of a feast in the making. I should have been changing into my best frock and getting ready to make merry, like every other witch and wizard in the world.

"Yes, I'm afraid Wizard Magigi has a preference for face to face communication."

"Alright." I couldn't have sounded more reluctant. I puffed my cheeks out. "I was so looking forward to everyone having a great Yuletide and Christmas this year," I lamented.

"I understand," Wizard Shadowmender replied, his voice soothing. "But look on the bright side."

"There's a bright side?"

"What time is it there?"

By habit, I glanced at the kitchen clock. I rolled my eyes. He'd tricked me. "Three fifty-eight. It feels like it's going to be three fifty-eight for the rest of my life. Permanently *not* dinnertime."

Yikes! What a thought!

Wizard Shadowmender's eyes sparkled. "Exactly! Here it's eight ..." he checked, "... thirty-four. Time continues to move on outside of Whittlecombe. All of your plans are merely on hold. Slightly delayed. Not cancelled."

"You mean we'll still have our party?"

"Once you've found out what you're dealing

with and put it right, time will catch up with itself, as is its habit."

Bah.

Once *you've* found out, he'd said. He was placing the onus all on me.

"I have every faith in you, so cheer up!" Wizard Shadowmender winked at me. "Now, I have to be at the Ministry of Witches for nine. Come up to London and seek out Wizard Magigi, Alf."

"Mah-jee-jee?" I repeated.

"Yes. You'll find him in a courtyard down Serendipity Way, a tiny alley that runs off Cross Lane."

"Cross Lane in Tumble Town?" I asked. I couldn't quite believe Wizard Shadowmender was sending me to the dark side.

"Yes, that Cross Lane. I really must go, Alf. My carriage awaits. Keep me posted. Ta-ta!"

"Wait—" I leaned forward and stared into the crystal of the orb. It clouded over. Bubbles formed and fermented, popped and dissipated.

He'd gone.

"Have a great time," I mumbled, only slightly sour.

"I have to go to London." I sat on the edge of my bed clutching Silvan's cool hand. I'd loosened his clothing and covered him in my quilt. "There's nobody here to look after things ... although—"

I glanced at the doorway where a huge Irish wolfhound was lying, sphinx-like, and staring at me through beautiful fiery gold eyes. How he'd managed to get inside the building was anybody's guess. I thought I'd secured all of the doors.

"—there's a bunch of dogs here. I hope this one that's guarding the bedroom door isn't hungry because he looks like he could devour you for breakfast."

The wolfhound snuffled. It sounded like a laugh. I regarded him warily, then squeezed Silvan's hand. "I'll close all the doors so that you're safe. At least you have Mr Hoo. Poor Charity is all alone next door. Wizard Shadowmender seemed to be saying that time will be held in limbo until we get this hex or curse or whatever it is lifted." I was rambling but I didn't really care. I just wanted him to hear my voice. "He called it a Somnus hex, or the Sleeping Beauty curse." I laughed, a little shakily. "A kind of reverse scenario, where it's the prince who's asleep and his princess"—I snorted at the thought of myself as a princess—"who does all the chasing around and tries to wake up her true love."

I folded his arm onto his chest then, deciding I didn't like what that pose symbolised, tucked it under the bedclothes instead. "So, I'm going to head up to London and have a word with Wizard Magigi, whoever he is, and hopefully find the cure and come back."

I smoothed his forehead. He didn't look remotely uneasy or concerned about anything. "You needn't worry about a thing." I could see he wasn't. "As far as you're concerned, it will be three fifty-eight until it isn't. And with any luck, I'll be back by then."

I stood up and bent over to kiss the top of his head where his brow met his hair. "I hope you're dreaming about me and not that blasted Maysoon," I whispered. Maysoon was a standing joke between us. Earlier this year, he'd made up a story about snuggling up with a camel in the desert whom he'd called Maysoon.

Reluctantly, I took my leave of him, moving towards the door. The Irish wolfhound moved out of the way to let me pass, but as I closed the door softly behind me, he lay back down and resumed his sphinx stance.

"Are you guarding my beloved?" I asked him,

and he thumped his tail against the wooden floorboards.

I pointed at the office door. "That's great. Can you look after Charity too?"

The tail thumped again.

I peered into the office. Charity hadn't moved. "I'll be back soon," I promised, "and I'll sort it. Don't worry."

I pulled the office door to and stared down at the dog. He gazed back at me, his eyes solemn. Did he genuinely understand what I was saying? On a whim, I crouched down and took a look at his collar. It didn't have his name, just the owner's surname. Warner.

"I wonder what your name is," I said, stroking his head. "I bet you're called something like Rajah or King or something mighty."

He wagged his tail again, more politely than enthusiastically this time.

"Thank you for looking after my friends," I told him. He bowed his head, then settled himself more comfortably.

Sighing, I made my way slowly down the back stairs and along the passage to the kitchen where several dogs were sniffing around the skirting boards on the lookout for crumbs.

I lifted the lid on the cauldron and eyed the broth, still simmering on the stove like Pease Porridge Hot. Should I turn everything off or leave it? Nothing *seemed* to be burning. Or even sticking to the pans. It simply remained at the same point in the cooking process as it had been when time stopped.

I decided to leave it. Chances were if everything reset while I was away from the inn, Monsieur Emietter and Florence would simply rush to put things right.

"Okeydokey. I'd better get going," I told the dogs. "Can you all stay out of mischief, do you think?"

"You can't possibly think that leaving these creatures here unattended is a sensible idea, Alfhild?"

The sound of my great-grandmother's voice shocked me so much my knees almost gave way. I whirled around to see her standing by the back door. I grabbed hold of the nearest counter to steady myself.

"By all that's green, Grandmama! You scared the calypso out of me."

"So I see." She watched as I pulled myself together. "You're off to London, I hear."

"Yes." I narrowed my eyes. "Have you been spying on me?"

"I wouldn't call it spying..."

"Why didn't you make yourself known to me?" I sounded irritated, but it was a mixture of frustration and relief to be fair.

Gwyn lifted her chin defensively. "You seemed to have everything in hand, my dear."

I pulled a face. "That really couldn't be further from the truth."

"Well, almost, perhaps." Gwyn floated forward and crouched down to get a better look at Monsieur Emietter. "This is most odd. I have heard of the Somnus hex but I've never seen it in action."

"I don't suppose you know how to undo it?" I asked hopefully. "Only, Silvan and Charity are fast asleep upstairs, and all the guests too. Tonight is supposed to be the Yule feast …" I trailed off, sounding as miserable as I felt.

"No, my dear. If I knew how to undo it, we wouldn't be having this conversation, would we?" old starchy-knickers replied. "But you've spoken to Wizard Shadowmender. You know what to do next." It was a statement rather than a question.

"So you haven't been here?" I surmised.

"No, indeed. Wizard Shadowmender alerted me to your latest shenanigans."

She had a knack of making everything sound like it was all my fault.

"He suggested you might find it agreeable to have some company."

Had she been with him in London? "Where were you?" I asked, then waved a hand. I knew she wouldn't tell me. "Never mind. The thing is, I'm just about to leave—"

"—for London, I know."

"He's recommended I speak to a Wizard—"

"Wizard Magigi. Serendipity Way. I know."

I resisted the urge to tell her that nobody likes a know-it-all and smiled sweetly instead. "But it *is* nice to have you back, Grandmama. Now that you're here, you could supervise the dogs for me," I suggested.

"I'm not a kennel maid, Alfhild. Have you opened an animal rescue in my absence?"

"You didn't know about Whittle Inn Canine Rescue?" I asked, affecting an air of total innocence. "Your great friend Wizard Shadowmender didn't let on?"

When her face creased with horror, I couldn't help but laugh. "Not at all. It's just I rescued—in a manner of speaking—Sunny and Jasper from Millicent's house, and then as I was walking home, we were joined by a few of their friends." I reached down to stroke the whippet, who had come to nuzzle against my legs. I was quite taken with her. "I've fed them all ... well ... there's an Irish wolfhound upstairs, I haven't fed him because I have no idea where he suddenly sprung from or how he got in—"

"Goodness gracious!" Gwyn slapped a hand to her forehead.

"He just turned up. So, they're mostly fed. Apart from that, I think you'll just need to let them out to attend to ... erm ... business before you bed down for the night—"

"It's out of the question, Alfhild."

"They'll need to go out!" I protested. "Think of the mess otherwise!"

"Why can't they sleep in the garden?" Gwyn asked. "They're dogs after all."

"People don't keep their dogs in the garden these days, Grandmama. And besides ... it's cold out there. It's sleeting. It would be cruel."

"So you intend to allow them free rein throughout the inn? That's preposterous."

"Just downstairs," I sought to reassure her. "I've filled up a few bowls of water and I'll give them some treats before I go, so it's just a matter of letting them out, and"—I thought I'd better spell it out for my crotchety old granny—"letting them *back in* again."

"As I said," Gwyn retorted, folding her arms, "it's out of the question."

"But Grandmama—"

"I'm coming with you, Alfhild."

My head jutted forward in surprise. "You're *what*?"

"You heard me. Grab your cloak and let's get going."

"I thought you would be driving, Alfhild." Gwyn pulled her scarf more firmly around her neck. We were waiting on the platform at Bristol Temple Meads for a train to London. Why are train stations the coldest places on the planet? The icy December wind blew right through my heavy robes and I shivered. Gwyn, being a ghost, couldn't feel the cold, but naturally she was milking the situation for all it was worth.

"All the way?" I queried. I'd parked Jed's van in the car park. Fortunately, it was quiet at this time of night and I hadn't had to fight for a space. "There's a congestion charge in the city which I would like to avoid paying. Plus, there's no parking to be had without taking out a mortgage. Not to mention the traffic. It's very different to your day."

"I'm sure you exaggerate, my dear."

"Not at all," I replied. "Believe me, it's easier this way."

A disembodied voice blared out of the speakers behind us. "The train approaching Platform 3 is the delayed twenty twenty-six to Birmingham New Street. Calling at—" I zoned the noise out and clapped my hands together to warm them up. A gentleman sitting on a bench to the right of me, clutching a large shopping bag containing lots of gaily wrapped presents, glanced at me warily. I smiled at him and turned back to my great-grand-mother, waiting for the station announcer to pipe down before speaking again.

"We'll get off at Paddington and then it's a quick Tube ride to Celestial Street."

"Are we at least travelling in first class?"

"No, Grandmama."

"Absurd," she sniffed. "I always travelled in first class when I took the train to London.

"Back in the days of steam locomotives," I muttered, and half-turned away from her, hoping she would take the hint and stop talking to me.

She didn't. "People are staring at you," she told me.

I widened my eyes in mock astonishment. "That's because they can't see you and they think I'm talking to myself!"

"Well, don't be so obvious about it. We don't want a doctor escorting you to an asylum somewhere."

I rolled my eyes. I'd be quite happy not to have to answer all her questions, but that was proving impossible. She was like an excitable child or a visitor from another planet. She wouldn't have admitted it, but I'd made her year by allowing her to accompany me on a trip.

Small things.

"What's that in those glass cases?" she was asking me now.

"Those are vending machines," I explained. "They have snacks in them. Crisps and chocolate and drinks and things."

"Oh, yes. We had those, I recall. Made of wood and brass. Much more tasteful from a design aesthetic. These are so much larger. Cheaper looking. More like the enormous refrigerators you have at the inn." She floated closer to the nearest one. "They hold so much. There must be a lot of food and milk spoiling in these."

This was not something I'd *ever* considered. "I suppose most products contain rather a lot of preservatives these days. And to be fair, there's probably a decent turnover of stock on a railway platform. And maybe the milk isn't actually fresh to begin with."

"Not fresh? Why would you want milk that wasn't fresh?" Gwyn huffed. "I don't know. It's all markedly different to my day. You know, once upon a time we kept cows at Whittle Inn. Perhaps you should—"

"Definitely not!"

"Oh." She studied the contents of the chocolate vending machine. "They're very pretty though, with all the lights. Don't you think?"

"Mmm-hmmm." I shot a look at the station clock, relieved that it at least did not say three fifty-eight. Would this train ever arrive? I fully intended to have a nap once we were safely onboard. I found myself wishing I'd brought some earplugs. Travelling with Gwyn was more exhausting than travelling with Florence.

Gwyn was studying the display. "What would you like, my dear? Something sweet?"

I hurriedly joined her. "You don't have any

money," I reminded her. "You have to put coins in the slot in order to buy the product."

"How much is it?" Modern money tended to confuse Gwyn. I had to do the Whittle Inn accounts two ways. Once in decimal, once pre-decimalisation.

I took a closer look. "It's one pound and twenty pence for a Twix," I pointed out.

"One pound? That's extortionate!" Before I could explain the cost to her—and to be fair, even I thought that was a stupid price to pay for a bar of chocolate-covered caramel and biscuit—she'd slid her hand and her head through the glass, as only a ghost can, and knocked a Twix into the dispensing tray.

"Grandmama!"

"There you are," she sang happily. "A little gift to you."

"You can't do that!" I hissed. "It's tantamount to stealing."

"At those prices, the company can afford it. They won't miss it."

I gave her my sternest look. "I can't believe you did that."

Her face fell as she thought better of it. "I suppose you're right. Put some coins in the slot, Alfhild. As you so kindly reminded me, I don't have any."

May the goddess preserve me. I dug around in my purse for some change. The next person would have a free chocolate bar on me.

"Perhaps you can get a cup of tea to go with it once we're on the train," Gwyn suggested.

I grumpily plucked the Twix from the tray and slid it into my pocket.

"We'll be lucky at this time of night," I said. Suddenly, Whittle Inn, my bed, Florence and a decent cuppa seemed a long way away.

Chapter Six

I had never seen Celestial Street so busy. The place teemed with merry revellers. Despite the lateness of the hour, all of the shops were taking advantage of the celebrations and remained open. Every window had been decorated beautifully. Lights sparkled; Yule hangings radiated seasonal warmth. As I pushed my way out of a bookshop's exit and into the main thoroughfare, a brass band—like an even more annoying version of the Devonshire Fellows—parped and tooted, making my ears vibrate with its deafening and unmelodic renditions of festive songs. In my hurry to get away from them, I stumbled into the path of a company of Morris Men, wearing crowns of twigs and holly, their faces daubed with green paint. They leapt and spun, their bells jangling, their clogs rapping on the cobbles. I feared for my toes, despite the fact that I'd encased them in a sturdy pair of heavy Dr Martens.

I made an attempt to sidle past the Morris Men, but their fool obstructed my path, waving his stick in my face. When I smiled—politely—and shifted left, he came with me, effectively blocking my way.

"Ha ha," I said, without much in the way of humour. It was nearly midnight after all, and I was on a mission. I side-stepped right. He came with me again.

My fingers curled around my wand, but Gwyn beat me to it.

She reprimanded him in her most disapproving voice. "Do get out of our way, you buffoon!"

He blinked at her in surprise. "My apologies, Madam."

"We're not here to party," she growled, "we have business!"

He stepped aside.

"Thank you, Grandmama," I said, and we hustled down the road a way, the scent of hot chestnuts, fried doughnuts, pork pies and sausages tantalising my senses. The Twix was burning a hole in my pocket and I wished I'd eaten it on the train, but there had been neither buffet car nor tea trolley and therefore nothing to wash it down. I'd napped, but now felt bleary-eyed and all the worse for it.

"Think nothing of it," Gwyn said, navigating the throng with ease while I was battered and jostled from all sides. "I've never trusted a man who wears bells."

I decided I was better off not knowing why.

Behind me the clock, in its tower atop the Ministry of Witches building, chimed the third quarter. Fifteen minutes to midnight. Fifteen minutes till the year turned back to the light in the northern hemisphere. The crowd around us was in a complete frenzy of excitement. From the corner of my eye I spotted sparks flying towards me. I ducked and whipped out my wand, but it turned out to be chocolate doubloons in gold foil wrappers. A witch in bright orange and red flowing robes and a sunny halo, balancing expertly on six-foot-high stilts, tossed the coins from a bucket to her adoring followers.

I managed to grab a couple before they tumbled to the ground and hurriedly peeled the foil away. I needed the sugar.

I spotted the right-hand turning into the narrow alleyway between two shops that led into Tumble Town. "This way," I told Gwyn, my mouth full. This was Cross Lane. At its widest, it was eight feet across. The houses bowed out at the top so that they almost met above my head, allowing little in the way of light down at ground level, even on a summer's day. I'd never visited Tumble Town after dark before. If I'd thought it a murky place on my previous visits, this trip did nothing to dispel such notions.

There weren't many streetlights, just the occasional muted lamp hanging from a building. Light glowed at a few of the windows, and that aided our passage, but for the most part we were trusting to luck that we wouldn't stumble through some hideous pool of ick or trip over some unfortunate vagabond or, perhaps tonight, a reveller who'd imbibed too much in the way of good cheer. I say 'we', but of course I mean me. Gwyn floated along effortlessly, not taking the slightest notice of my complaints whenever I stubbed a toe, trod in something squidgy or scraped my knuckles against a building.

We passed numerous tiny shops on both sides. Unlike the jolly shopfronts in Celestial Street, these were grimy windows with shutters and old lace curtains, or meagre window displays. Carpenters, seamstresses, tailors, a cobbler, a wandmaker, a potionery, a tiny pet shop. I shuddered to think what sort of dark and demonic pets you might find inside there, malformed and discontented.

I didn't stop to look.

Unlike my visits in the daytime, I was surprised by how busy Tumble Town appeared to be. I suppose I shouldn't have been really. This small town had grown up behind the official hub of British witch society to house those witches, wizards and warlocks, mages and sages, fae folk and other paranormal creatures who preferred to operate outside of the Ministry of Witches' jurisdiction. It seemed odd to me that such people would prefer to remain in plain sight of those they professed to hate, but for their part, the Ministry of Witches seemed happy enough to co-reside with their darker counterparts and overlook any mild transgressions.

Tumble Town is where Silvan came from. Where he belonged. Bless his little dark heart.

People hugged the shadows as I hurried past. Here and there, unnatural eyes glowed out of shallow doorways, watching me, appraising me as a potential danger or a victim no doubt. I drew up the hood of my cloak, suddenly feeling self-conscious down here, so late at night. Someone close by snickered, a malicious throaty ripple. Nerves fluttered in my stomach.

"Pfft." I heard Gwyn's soft explosion of disdain. "Mischief makers, nothing more, Alfhild. Nothing to fear here."

I kept going, thankful for my great-grandmother's presence, averting my eyes from those who strolled towards us and grateful for the candles that burned in the windows and helped to light our way. Deeper and deeper we walked into Cross Lane. Occasionally, rather than watching where I was stepping, I had to lift my head to scrutinise the gold letters on the small black iron signs at the entrance to yet another alley, hopeful for a clue as to our whereabouts. Tumble Town was a maze of such alleys and tiny winding streets. Not enough room for vehicles; perhaps a horse and carriage if you were lucky, but generally the widest transport you'd come across would be a laden donkey.

Not tonight, though.

Tonight was a night for the shadow people.

We arrived in a courtyard, the lighting better here. To my left was Knick-Knack Lane. Walk down there and you'd find The Web and Flame where I'd first encountered Silvan.

"We need to turn right," Gwyn said, and so I followed her, reluctant to leave the security of the courtyard for an even darker thoroughfare than Cross Lane. Even The Web and Flame, usually chock-full of rogues and roustabouts, would have felt like a sanctuary this evening.

We hadn't gone far when Gwyn stopped and pointed up. I surveyed a sign on the brickwork, several feet above my head. Serendipity Way. We'd reached our destination. I turned into the impossibly thin, bricked alley, ducking to avoid smacking my forehead against the heavy lintel that framed the entrance, and found myself in another courtyard, the ground paved with uneven and incredibly old cobblestones. Several workshops, closed up and heavily shuttered, faced out into the yard, along with four small shops. These seemed meticulously kept, the window frames in good repair, the glass, from what I could make out, clean. Lights were on in three of the shops, but muted, as though they were on timer switches, designed to go out at midnight.

I faltered, afraid that we'd travelled all of this way and the shop was closed, but Gwyn drifted past me.

"This one," she said.

Gold letters had been stencilled across the glass window: *Mr Magigi's Magickal Emporium*.

I joined Gwyn at the window and stared at the display. At first glance, the array of objects looked like so much junk. But on closer inspection I could see this wasn't the case. Ornately carved wands, some of them dating from medieval times, Victorian tear catchers, a battered top hat, a vampire's mirror, goblets, handblown potion bottles, a herbalist's miniature cabinet, a compendium of magickal children's games. I was particularly taken with a large, old-fashioned black camera with a leather case. I wondered what the story was there.

Everything had evidently been pre-owned. Wizard Magigi was a dealer of witchy antiques by the look of things. No wonder he hid out in the bowels of Tumble Town. I would bet my last shilling that there were some oddities and curiosities hidden away in the back of his shop that the Ministry of Witches would take a particularly dim view of.

Intriguing.

I longed to have a root around but for now, we were here with a single purpose.

"Is it open?" I asked. The lighting inside was subdued. There appeared to be nothing moving.

"There's only one way to find out, Alfhild." My great-grandmother stated the obvious. "Open the door, child."

"Alright!" I bit back the testiness in my voice. I was tired—it had been a long day—and tetchy because I was missing my party even while everyone in Celestial Street appeared to be having the time of their lives.

Away from Celestial Street, here in Tumble Town, celebrations were a little more muted but music and raucous voices travelled through the still night, and I imagined the pubs and taverns were jammed full of revellers.

I pushed against the door with the flat of my hand. At first, it didn't budge, but with a little more force it juddered and creaked open. The tinkling of the bell above our heads announced our arrival. I stepped inside, glad of the warmth, my senses assaulted by the amazing array of goods lining the shelves, the colours and of course, the smell. Mr Magigi's Magickal Emporium had that same fustiness I so loved in Whittlecombe's post office. The smell of old paper and dust mixed with a bit of damp and a sense of history.

The Emporium was a relatively small shop, perhaps sixteen feet wide and thirty deep. I pushed back the hood of my robes so that I could see better. The floor had been left uncovered and comprised plain wooden floorboards. The shelves themselves were unfussy. They lined the walls above purpose-built cabinets containing dozens of neat drawers with brass shell-shaped handles. In the centre of the shop floor was another large shelving unit, in a kind of A shape. This one was laden with larger objects: hand-carved wooden dolls, skulls, an enormous stuffed bird whose black eyes glittered in the light. A gigantic jawbone, from a whale or something similar, hung from the ceiling along with half a dozen stained glass orb lampshades, the bulbs emitting the orange hue of subdued lighting.

There were more shelves at the rear, nestled behind a wide counter that took up the whole length of the shop. An old wooden till, little more than a rectangular box, the kind without any sort of numeric display, had been arranged on one side of the counter. The opposite end, most peculiar of all, was dominated by a tree that appeared to have grown out of the floor. The tree's canopy disappeared above the height of the ceiling and was lost from view, almost as though the tree had been here first and the shop premises had been built around it. The counter had been cut in such a way as to accommodate the tree. Some of its lower branches swept out towards the shop. Directly beneath it, on the counter, was a large fruit bowl, brimming with grapes, bananas, peaches, strawberries and mangoes, most of it out of season and gloriously fresh and colourful, and oddly incongruous for a shop in dark and dingy Tumble Town.

Despite the jangle of the bell, nobody sallied forth to greet us. I could have walked off with half the stock if I'd wanted to—if I'd known what use any of it was—and nobody would have bothered.

I cleared my throat, hoping Wizard Magigi would be close by and hear.

Still no-one appeared, although I heard a rustle emanating from the tree. I waited a few seconds, aware of Gwyn's mounting ire. "Wizard Magigi?" I called politely.

Something whizzed through the air and struck me on the ear before falling to the floor. "Ow!"

I glanced down. A grape. As I looked up, another one flew past me.

"Look, Alfhild." Gwyn directed my attention towards the tree. I spotted a monkey, camouflaged by the foliage to some extent, with creamy-gold fur over its body and a black face.

"Wow!" I breathed. "What a little cutey! Such astonishing eyes!" Its eyes were a bright, intelligent blue. It observed me keenly, as though it could fully understand what I was saying. This could well be Wizard Magigi's familiar, I decided. If it was, it wouldn't thank me for being called cute. On the off chance, I addressed it directly.

"Greetings! My name is Alfhild Daemonne and this is my great-grandmother, erm, also Alfhild Daemonne." Gwyn shot me a glance that I interpreted to mean she thought I had sabotaged a great name. "We're seeking an audience with Wizard Magigi on Wizard Shadowmender's recommendation."

The monkey, clinging to a branch with one arm, swung itself so that its other arm could scoop up some fruit. I'd hardly had time to blink and it had launched another grape directly at me, hitting me square on the nose. "Hey!" I blinked in stunned surprise.

"Do shut the door," the monkey said. "You're letting all the warm air out."

I gaped at the monkey, but when it took aim with another grape, I quickly closed my mouth and retreated to the door, hurriedly pushing it closed, remembering to add a little force to prevent it sticking.

"I apologise," I said, sneaking a wary look back at

the monkey, hoping it wasn't going to pelt me with any more fruit. I rubbed my nose ruefully. "I should imagine where you come from"—I didn't know an awful lot about monkeys and quickly realised I was going to put my ignorance centre stage—"it's warmer than the UK."

The monkey stared at me without blinking. "Where I'm from?" it repeated. "I was born *here*. In this very tree."

Oh, good grief. I really needed to stop talking. "You were?"

"I was." The monkey plucked another grape and I got ready to duck, but it hauled itself onto a branch, settled itself comfortably and started to peel the skin of the fruit away.

I relaxed a little. "We were looking for Wizard Magigi?" I prompted it.

"Were you indeed?" the monkey asked, sucking the grape into its mouth and dropping the skin onto the counter below. "And what did you want with him? He's extremely busy."

I glanced doubtfully at the door. I could hear the distant sound of fireworks. It would be just my luck that we'd come all this way and Wizard Magigi was out on the town having a skinful of ale. No doubt he'd be too inebriated to talk to us any time soon.

"Time's a-pressing," Gwyn reminded me.

I sucked in a breath. The monkey had to be some sort of gatekeeper. I'd have to tell it my story and then explain the whole thing again to the wizard. But what else could I do? "I've come from Whittle Inn in East Devon. Earlier today—at three fifty-eight to be precise—the village of Whittlecombe fell under some sort of hex. A Somnus hex, we believe—"

"Ah, yes. The Sleeping Beauty curse," the monkey nodded. "Go on."

"That's right. Everyone in the vicinity as far as I could make out, all the villagers, all the ghosts that work at my inn, my guests, my manager and my boyfriend, they're all fast asleep."

"I see," the monkey replied, wiping its paws on a leaf.

"Wizard Shadowmender, the head of my coven—"

"I know Shadowmender," the monkey interrupted again.

"You do?" That surprised me. "Well, anyway, he suggested Wizard Magigi might be able to help."

"Why would he suggest that?" The monkey was certainly anything *but* helpful.

"I don't know really," I replied, and this time the frustration was evident in my voice. I sounded cranky. "Why don't you tell me where I can find him and then I can ask him?"

The monkey regarded me through its piercing blue eyes. There was a long, drawn-out silence where I had the time to reflect on my bad manners.

"I'm sorry," I said. "I didn't mean to be rude."

The monkey smiled. Its teeth were as dazzling as its eyes. "Apology accepted." It swung from the branch of the tree, elongating its body. From the point where its hands clasped the branch to the tip of its tail, it must have been way over a metre in length. It dropped lightly to the counter and hopped forwards into a crouch to take a better look at me.

"Why do you assume you haven't already found him?" the monkey asked.

Gwyn made a soft noise beside me.

My chin jutted forward in shock. "*You're* Wizard Magigi?"

"The very same."

I groaned inwardly. *How to make friends and influence people.*

"I do apologise," I said again, dashing my hand against my forehead. "I'm an idiot."

"You can say that again," Gwyn chipped in. "We're so very pleased to make your acquaintance,

Wizard Magigi." She swept forwards and inclined her head gracefully.

"I really didn't mean to insult you." I couldn't have felt worse.

Wizard Magigi waved his monkey paw at me, dismissing my concerns. "You wouldn't be the first. It amuses me." He studied my face. "You look tired. One moment." He leaned backwards and directed his voice at a gap in the shelving to the side of the counter. "Nadim!" he called. A few seconds later a man in his fifties, short in stature and with dark, neatly cropped hair and a smart moustache, wearing a beautiful red waistcoat embroidered with golden thread, pushed through the beaded curtain and appeared at the wizard's side.

"Sir?" Nadim asked.

"We have guests." Wizard Magigi indicated us. Nadim smiled at us. "Please bring a chair and some tea for Ms Daemonne."

Nadim bowed and retreated.

"That's very kind," I said.

"And Mrs Daemonne? Is there anything I can provide for your comfort?" Wizard Magigi wanted to know.

Gwyn shook her head. "I am perfectly happy, thank you."

Nadim brought out a chair and placed it in front of the counter. I plonked myself into it. It gave Wizard Magigi an advantage, for now I had to look up at him. That seemed rather fitting under the circumstances. I settled myself, and the tea followed seconds later. Nadim brought out a tray with a large silver teapot, a matching sugar bowl and a pair of glasses full to the brim with green leaves.

"Mint tea," Nadim told me when I studied my glass doubtfully. "Refreshing."

"Perfect," I said. I'd never had authentically brewed mint tea before, so this would be a first. Nadim lifted the teapot and poured the golden liquid into the glass from quite a height. I watched, entranced. He was unerringly accurate and didn't splash a drop.

Don't try this at home, I reminded myself.

Nadim handed me the sugar bowl. "Sugar to taste," he told me. "Sweet is good." With that, he bowed once more and disappeared.

"Tell me everything," Wizard Magigi ordered.

I took a sip from the glass. The combination of fresh mint, sugar and strong tea was quite glorious. I felt instantly soothed and warmed through. I relaxed a little in my chair.

"It's all a bit curious," I began by saying.

Wizard Magigi plucked a grape from the nearby fruit bowl. I noticed that no matter how many of these he ate, and he ate a lot, there always seemed to be the same amount.

"Splendid," said Wizard Magigi. "I do enjoy curiosities."

CHAPTER SEVEN

I finished the story of what I'd done, and where I'd been and who I'd talked to and what I'd seen and what I hadn't found out at precisely the same time as I finished my tea.

Wizard Magigi had listened to the whole sorry tale from beginning to end and then made me repeat it. He'd asked me a few questions to clarify one or two points and seemed particularly interested in the characters I'd mentioned along the way.

"Silvan?" he'd queried.

"My boyfriend. He hails from Tumble Town himself. Horace T Silvanus," I elucidated. "You may know him."

I couldn't tell from Wizard Magigi's face whether he recognised the name or not. He gave nothing away. His whiskers didn't even twitch.

He'd also been interested in the postmaster, and Stan and Rhona in Whittle Stores. Finally, he asked to see the box. I drew the small, square, intricately carved item out of my bag and handed it over.

He reached into the fruit bowl and, after a quick rummage, revealed a monocle that he popped over his right eye. Taking the box between his front paws, he turned it round and round, inspecting it from all angles, tracing the carvings with a long nail on his right paw. He opened the box, scrutinised the lid and sniffed the velvet.

"You said that you heard no birdsong?" Wizard Magigi asked.

"That's right. Perhaps I wouldn't have heard much, given the time of day, but generally you can still hear the crows and robins, and sometimes even seagulls when they've come inland a little."

"And there were no cats around?"

"None," I confirmed. "Just the dogs I told you about."

"Intriguing."

Wizard Magigi closed the lid of the box and pushed it away. "May I see the wrappings the box was delivered in?"

"There was no note," I reminded him, but I rooted around in my bag, found the brown paper wrappings and handed them over.

The wizard smoothed out the crumpled paper and read the address. "It seems to me that the fact that this wasn't addressed to anyone specific is particularly pertinent," he said.

"Why?" I asked.

"Besides yourself, who might have collected the parcel from the post office?"

I didn't need to think. "Only my manager, Charity. But she wouldn't have opened it."

"Exactly. It had to be you, because whoever cast the hex wanted someone close to you to be affected."

"Why not just send it directly to Alfhild at Whittle Inn?" Gwyn asked. "Why send it to the post office?"

Wizard Magigi wobbled his head. "My best guess would be that the person who sent it doesn't know Whittlecombe or Whittle Inn. Perhaps they don't even know Ms Daemonne. They loaded up this hex to affect a large area in the hope they would find their target."

"You're saying my great-granddaughter was *not* the target?" Gwyn raised her eyebrows.

I was taken aback. Not that I'd even considered that I *was* a target. I think I'd assumed that my wonky inn had been. There were people everywhere who would be happy to see the inn fail, but then again … most of them were neighbouring landowners such as Gladstone Talbot-Lloyd and the innkeeper of the local competition, The Hay Loft's Lyle Cavendish. I couldn't see either of them employing any kind of hex.

They wouldn't have known where to start.

Wizard Magigi plucked another grape from the bowl. "No, but somebody close to her was."

"Who then?" There weren't that many people I was close to.

Wizard Magigi shrugged. "I can't answer that." He pulled the box towards himself. "I'll tell you what I do know, if you're interested?"

"Of course!" I leaned forward.

"Whoever did this is an amateur."

I jerked backwards. "Are you sure? I mean, they've knocked out an entire village!"

"I'm absolutely sure. They did indeed, as you say, knock out a village—but it was by luck, not judgement. They couldn't have known where or when you would open that parcel. The most they would have hoped for was that you were at the inn, but you weren't."

"Alright," I said. I didn't find that information particularly useful.

"My second observation is that this person likes dogs."

I blinked. "Pardon?"

"The fact that the local dogs have not been affected by the hex leads me to surmise that they have been purposefully omitted."

"You mean it was written into the hex that—"

"—no dogs would be hurt in the undertaking of the magick," Wizard Magigi confirmed.

I pulled a face. "So, I'm looking for someone who is an amateur magician or witch who loves dogs." That didn't exactly narrow the field.

Wizard Magigi fixed me with those intense eyes of his. "You're approaching this the wrong way."

I cocked my head. He had my attention. "Go on."

"You were also excluded from the hex and there has to be a reason for that too."

"Of course," Gwyn muttered. "We should have thought of that."

"Whether you were excluded inadvertently, I really can't say." Wizard Magigi peeled his latest grape.

"So I might have been left out on purpose or I might not have been?" I narrowed my eyes. This was all as clear as mud.

"Exactly." He discarded the skin of the grape and reached for another one. "I'm thinking that whoever cast this hex wants it to be undone. If you can figure out who the target actually was, you'll be better placed to undo it." He clasped his paws together. "Why was the parcel to be opened immediately?"

"I assumed it was a Yule gift," I told him.

"Never make assumptions. What else is special about today?"

I cast around, trying to think. "I don't know … it's the shortest day … we are—were—will be—having a party. Who knows? Lots of baking … erm … a bonfire … ah … an inn full of guests who arrived for the festivities … wait!" I sat bolt upright. "Silvan. It's Silvan. He arrived back today."

Wizard Magigi nodded in satisfaction.

"I've been bleating on about it for weeks. Everyone knew he would be at home—well, with me at the inn—all over Yule and Christmas. I've been so excited …" I trailed off. How typical that Silvan should be at the centre of this. "Does it have something to do with his job?" I asked. "Because if it does, I have no hope of ever getting to the bottom of it. He doesn't talk to me about what he does. Anything I do know, I've found out only when our lives have collided."

I thought back to the Silvan-Bill escapade and experienced a little frisson of excitement. That had been fun. In the end. The Meztli episode, not so much.

Wizard Magigi's gaze dropped back to the box. "It strikes me that for the person who cast the hex, part of their enjoyment is going to come from watching you trying to work out the puzzle. They probably don't want harm to come to Silvan, otherwise they would have found another way."

I felt cheered by this.

"It's difficult to know what their motive is, however," he continued, opening the box and scrutinising the insides again, "but they will want you to solve the mystery. Of that, I'm sure."

"How will—"

Wizard Magigi hooked a sharp nail into the velvet material inside and tugged. The velvet remained stubbornly where it was for a moment, resisting. He pulled harder and worked the fabric free, dropping it to the counter along with a tiny square of vellum. "Aha!"

I leaned forwards. "What's that? A note?"

"A clue." Wizard Magigi adjusted his monocle.

"Let me see …" He hooked his long, curved claw beneath the paper and flipped it over. "Just three words," he said. "True Love's Kiss."

"True love's kiss?" I repeated. "What sort of clue is that?"

Gwyn was faster on the uptake than me. "I suppose it's not called the Sleeping Beauty Curse for no reason, is it my dear?"

"You're saying Silvan can be awoken with a kiss?" I asked, my voice sounding oddly flat.

"It's worth a try," Wizard Magigi replied.

"But what about everyone else?" Gwyn asked. "Charity and the villagers?"

"And the ghosts?" I added.

Gwyn nodded. "Does she have to kiss everyone?"

"I'd struggle to kiss the ghosts," I said. *And would I really have to kiss Finbarr? Bleugh! I'd certainly draw the line at his pixies.*

Wizard Magigi's blue eyes flashed. "Perhaps you'll start a chemical reaction," he said, enunciating every word.

I stared at him, wondering what I was missing.

He held up the carved trinket box. "When you've finished with this, may I have it?"

I checked with Gwyn. I couldn't see any reason

why I needed to keep it in the long term. She shrugged and nodded.

"Be my guest," I said.

"Consider it outstanding payment for services rendered." He rummaged in the fruit bowl and drew out a wand. "*Invenient me!*" he told it, then handed it back to me.

"Thank you," I said.

He nodded and reached up with one of his long arms, stretching to grab a low branch, and hauled himself back into his tree. "Good day to you," he said.

"Wait," I called, but he'd disappeared. Camouflaged by the leaves, he'd already climbed above the height of the ceiling.

Nadim appeared at my elbow and politely held out his hand for my glass. I handed the empty vessel over to him. He led the way to the door and pulled it open. He obviously had a knack. It slid noiselessly wide.

Gwyn and I passed through, back into the cool outside air, the sparkling rain, with hints of ice quickly coating my robes.

"Thank you," I said to Nadim. He bowed and pushed the door closed. The bell tinkled prettily.

I pulled up the hood of my cloak, watching as

Nadim turned the sign on the door from open to closed.

Our encounter with Wizard Magigi was over.

Now we had to figure out what to do next.

CHAPTER EIGHT

One of the advantages of Tumble Town is that the businesses there operate outside the realms of the law, both those of the mundane world and those enacted by the Ministry of Witches. And so it was that, at nearly one in the morning, I found myself tucked into a corner seat in The Web and Flame.

Hidden away down Knick-Knack Lane, The Web and Flame was a real old-fashioned spit and sawdust London pub, with roughly hewn wooden benches and worn wooden tables. A proper den of iniquity, it was frequented by ruffians and vagabonds, warlocks and sorcerers, witches and wizards who were down on their luck, or simply plain bad.

Not forgetting Silvan, of course.

On the first occasion I'd visited, I'd been amazed

by how lacking in cheer I'd found it to be, but perhaps that had been due in large part to my frame of mind at the time. Now, I figured, this pub could be counted as any port in a storm.

I huddled miserably against the wall, nursing a glass of Hoodwinker. Gwyn, 'perching' on the bench opposite me, watched as I swirled the liquid around in the glass.

"I really don't know what the matter is, Alfhild. I assumed you'd want to be on the first train out of London."

"To rush back to my beau, you mean?" I sighed. "Mmm."

"Well, yes?" Gwyn sounded confused.

I decided to change the subject. "Did you know that Wizard Magigi was a monkey?"

"I did not," Gwyn said. "I had heard tell of a monkey wizard, but I'd never met him before. Quite fascinating."

"Do you think he's a monkey because he's been cursed?"

Gwyn frowned. "I know as much as you, my dear. Very little."

"He may be a shifter, of course," I mused.

"That's a possibility too." Gwyn pointed at my glass. "Drink up. I think we should go home."

"Why should we go home?" I growled, surprising myself with the catch in my voice.

"Why ... you're not crying are you, Alfhild? What on earth is wrong?" Gwyn reached out as though she would pat my hand. I wished she could.

"Don't you see, Grandmama?" I said, blinking back the sudden tears in my eyes. "Silvan has to be awoken by a true love's kiss."

"Exactly! That's why we need to go home." Gwyn wafted her hands at me. "Come on. I don't understand why you're prevaricating."

"I already kissed him!" I told her. My voice sounded loud, even in the general hubbub of the crowded pub. A few people turned to look at me. I lowered my voice and my gaze. "I kissed him before I left."

Gwyn stared at me, not quite comprehending.

"If my kiss could have woken him up, he'd already be awake."

"I don't think—"

"Do you know what that means?" I wailed. "Do you?"

"Alfhild—"

"It means I'm not his true love!"

I burst into tears.

"Balderdash." Gwyn had let me snuffle into my beer for long enough. She had obviously grown tired of waiting for me to sort myself out because now she drew herself up and fixed me with a stern eye.

"B-b-but I k-k-kissed him," I repeated. "If I-hi-hi was h-h-his true—"

"If I thought for even one second that you and he weren't supposed to be together, believe me I would never have let him anywhere near Whittle Inn after the first time. He's a grand young man. A little unconventional, a teeny bit fragrant at times—"

"Th-th-that's the camels," I told her.

"I'm aware of this, my dear, but they have wells even in remote regions of Bezspeckispystan or wherever the blazes he ends up. The man could wash."

"Maybe he wants to blend in," I replied, indignant *despite* that fact that he evidently loved someone more than me.

That thought set me off again and I snuffled and snorted.

"Don't you carry a handkerchief?" my great-grandmother asked in despair. Quick as a flash, she darted off to retrieve some paper serviettes and sprinkled them over my head. "Here. Dry your eyes and wipe your nose."

I did as she suggested, and took a long glug of Hoodwinker for good measure. It calmed me down a little.

"So what are you going to do?" Gwyn enquired when I had dried up.

I sighed and slumped over my beer.

"Shoulders back, Alfhild. It's all about mind over matter. Act strong and confident to be strong and confident."

I accepted the rebuke and sat up properly. She was right, of course.

"What can I do? Silvan is only one part of the puzzle. I have to wake him, presumably, in order to wake up everyone else. And besides"—I swallowed the lump that had formed in my throat once more—"he may not love me the way that I love him, but I still want to do right by him."

Gwyn nodded with evident satisfaction. "Spoken like a true Daemonne."

"I may not be the love of his life, but she's out there somewhere." I lifted my chin. "And I'll find her and take her to him."

"I like the cut of your gib," Gwyn said. "But how do we find this person?"

That stumped me. I rolled back the various conversations Silvan and I had shared about our pasts. He was a strange mix of open and frank while simultaneously playing his cards close to his chest. I knew he'd had several relationships, but who with was anybody's guess.

"I wouldn't know where to start," I admitted.

A blast of cold air swept around the pub as someone came in from outside. There were calls and jeers, people demanding the door be closed. I looked up to see a cloaked man wobble around on his axis. He'd evidently been partying hard and was a little worse for wear, but that didn't stop him wanting a nightcap. I was reminded of how I'd first met Silvan here in this very room and how, when I'd wanted to track him down again, I had come here.

And nobody had helped me ...

But somehow word had reached him ...

And a small girl had waylaid me in the narrow lane outside and directed me to Marissa's dwelling.

Marissa.

I hadn't seen her for a while, and she had always denied that she and Silvan were anything more than friends, but I'd hazard a guess that even were that the case, she would know a little more about his recent romantic past than I would.

And if that was so, I could work backwards. Trace his previous girlfriends. One by one if necessary.

Gwyn narrowed her eyes. "What's going on in that busy mind of yours, Alfhild? I can see you're concocting a plan. I do hope it's a good one?"

"So do I," I said. "So do I."

Chapter Nine

The first time I'd visited Marissa's first floor apartment, where Silvan had been staying at the time, I'd walked miles even though I hadn't needed to. The whole thing had been a wild goose chase because actually, Marissa lived literally around the corner from The Web and Flame.

I led Gwyn down the alleys, pausing to get my bearings until I recognised the tiny inlet between the buildings that led to a rickety and winding wooden staircase. This took us up past several battered doors and along a kind of veranda until I found the correct front door. Fortunately, a dim light emanated from the foot of the entrance. Marissa, or somebody, was awake inside.

I tapped gently on the door, hoping I wouldn't disturb any of her neighbours, and waited. I heard shuffling and a muffled voice, then silence.

I tapped again. "Marissa?" I hissed in as loud a whisper as I could manage.

More muffled words, then footsteps in the hall. The door was pulled open, slowly, and Marissa's pale face stared out at me in surprise.

"It's me," I whispered, then, in case she didn't immediately recognise me, "Alf."

"Alf?" Marissa's smooth, beautiful face creased into a frown. "What are you doing here?"

"It's a long story."

Marissa pulled the door open further and stepped out, looking about. "Where's Silvan?"

"That's why I'm here. Why we're here." I indicated Gwyn. "We really need to talk to you. May we come in?"

Marissa hesitated. I'd heard her talking through the door. Did that mean she had company? I shouldn't have assumed it was alright to call on her at this time of night.

I fidgeted awkwardly. "I'm sorry. If it's not convenient—" I stepped backwards.

Marissa shook her head. "Don't be silly. If it's about Silvan—"

She stepped back, away from the door. "Please, come in."

I followed her inside and closed the door after myself.

"Excuse the mess," Marissa was saying. She led us through into her small living room. I remembered all the plants and the pretty light wicker furniture. Perfect for a hot Tumble Town summer; somehow odd in the middle of winter. Yet Marissa gave off the impression that it was permanently summer. Not a fae, I'd often wondered whether she was distantly related to one because she had such a light elegance. She was tall, impossibly slender, and wore loose-flowing, weightless clothing. Her wavy hair, long and blonde, seemed bleached by the sun even here in the dark and dismal backwaters of Tumble Town. Her skin and eyes glowed with pale but vital health. She was an enigma and, being as nosy as I was, I wanted to know more.

Perhaps now I had the chance to find out.

"It's just I have my niece staying with me." She indicated a small, dark-eyed child with hair as long and white as Marissa's own, sitting cross-legged on a rug in the centre of the room, surrounded by vacant-eyed dolls, forlorn soft toys, board games, scattered plastic game pieces and crumpled wads of fake cash. "This is Gertie," Marissa said. "She's six. My sister's child."

"Hi!" I said brightly.

The child curled her lip in disdain. "Who are you?" she asked with a level of malevolence I found unnerving in one so young.

"This is Alfhild Daemonne, Gertie. She lives in a big inn in Devon. Near the seaside."

"You can call me Alf," I told her. I turned and indicated Gwyn. "And this is my great-grandmother. You can call her—"

"—Mrs Daemonne," Gwyn chipped in.

The little girl's eyes widened. "Are you a—?"

"A ghost? That's correct," Gwyn responded, her tone crisp.

"Wow!" The child seemed excited by this. "I've never met a ghost before."

"You should come and stay at our inn sometime," I suggested, more to be polite than anything else. "We have dozens of ghosts."

"Why would I want to stay at your stinky inn?" Gertie looked most perturbed by the idea.

"I, er, well ..." I didn't quite know what to say to that. I suppose it wasn't particularly child friendly unless that child was interested in climbing trees and playing games on the lawn. *Fair point*, I conceded.

"Perhaps it's time for you to go to bed, Gertie?"

Marissa suggested, and I heard a note of longing in her voice. Maybe she'd been having a long day too.

"I told you I don't want to!"

"But you must be tired," Marissa coaxed. "Alf and I need to have a little chat."

"I don't care! I want to stay up all night." Gertie screwed her face up and I feared for a moment she would have a tantrum.

"I don't understand why you want to stay up all night. You'll be exhausted tomorrow." Marissa's voice remained calm and quiet. She had the patience of a saint.

"It's none of your business!" Gertie shrieked. I looked on in terror. She'd devoured too many e-numbers through the course of the day, I decided.

"Gertie," Marissa lowered her voice even further. "There's no need to be so rude in front of our guests."

Gertie glared at me. "They're not our guests. We didn't invite them here."

Marissa might be Gertie's blood kin, but her grace and elegance obviously didn't run in the family.

I could feel the electric vibration of Gwyn's displeasure. The air positively bristled. I hurriedly fixed a smile to my face, not wanting Gwyn to say anything *I'd* end up regretting. "It's fine, Marissa. I can see you're busy—"

"Take a seat, Alf," Marissa responded, her voice firm. "You came here for a reason and it must be important. Gertie *will* play quietly while you and I talk." She indicated one of the wicker seats and, reluctantly, I sat down.

Gertie poked her tongue out at me and went back to playing with her dolls.

"What brings you here?" Marissa asked, her voice low.

I quickly ran through the events of the day—actually the previous day now, although given that I hadn't been to sleep it all seemed to be merging into one for me—and explained how I'd opened the mysterious box at the post office and that had been the catalyst that sent everyone to sleep.

"So I've left everyone slumbering at Whittle Inn with only a pack of dogs to look out for them."

"La la la la!" Gertie started to sing loudly. Startled, I stopped speaking.

"Gertie?" Marissa held out a finger. "Hush, darling." She nodded at me. "Go on, Alf."

"I spoke to Wizard Shadowmender—"

"La la la la la!" I had no idea what tune Gertie was trying to sing, but it grated.

"—and he recommended I come to Tumble Town—"

"La la la la la!"

"—and connect with Wizard Magigi down Serendipity Way—"

"La la la la la!"

Gwyn tutted loudly. I widened my eyes at her. Have a little patience, Grandmama, I telegraphed.

"Oh yes, I know Mister Magigi. He does stock some enchanting items," Marissa said. "Hush, Gertie."

"I showed him the box, and that's what brought me to you."

"La la la la la!"

"Why?" Marissa looked confused. To be honest, I probably hadn't explained myself very well. I could hardly hear myself think.

"Because, when he pulled apart the lining in the box, a slip of paper fell out—"

"La la—" Gertie stopped singing, ducking her head to examine something on the doll's body. Perhaps she'd wrenched the arm out of its socket or something, or disembowelled it. I wouldn't put anything past this charming kid.

"It said 'true love's kiss', which Wizard Magigi

suggested meant that Silvan at least could be woken up with a kiss."

"How very Sleeping Beauty," said Marissa. She held my eye and smiled. "I'm still not sure why you came here."

I took a deep breath. It hurt to say it. "I already kissed Silvan. He didn't wake up."

Gertie giggled. I stared at my hands. The room fell completely silent.

I let the facts sink in.

"Kissing is icky," Gertie offered.

"Mind your own business, Gertie," Marissa said, her tone sharper than before. She reached out and took my hand. "Alf, I'm sorry."

I nodded, unable to find words.

"But you know,"—she glanced at Gertie—"he and I, we have never been anything except friends."

I lifted my head to look at her. How could Silvan not have fallen in love with this beautiful, kind-hearted woman? It seemed impossible to me.

"He stays here," Gertie volunteered.

"From time to time." Marissa looked slightly uncomfortable.

"He was here the other night," Gertie told me.

I started in surprise. "Was he?"

"He'd flown in from somewhere, late," Marissa

explained hurriedly. "He needed somewhere to crash before he travelled down to you."

I nodded. This seemed likely.

Gertie giggled again. "He's fun." She yanked her doll by the hair and its head came off.

I felt a pang of regret for the poor doll. I knew how she felt. "Yes, he is." I looked back up at Marissa.

She shrugged. "It's not me he loves," she repeated.

"You say that," I said, "but what if it is? How well do we ever know another person? What if the flame burns deeply inside of you? Inside you both? Isn't it just possible?"

"I …" Marissa pulled a face. "Of course, it's possible, but I just can't see it myself."

"I came here to ask you to come back to the inn with me," I told her. "You know I would try anything."

Marissa indicated Gertie. "You can see my situation."

I nodded. "I know. I can't expect—"

"I'll come," Gertie piped up. "Let's go." She stood up, kicked her broken doll aside and grabbed one of the soft toys instead. I feared for its life. "I like doggies."

I grunted. You wouldn't be able to hide much from this little girl.

"I don't think that's a good idea, Gertie." Marissa hurriedly jumped to her feet. "You need to go to bed."

Gertie began to shriek. "I don't want to go to bed!"

"It sounds to me like you should have gone hours ago," Gwyn said. "Why on earth did you want to stay up?"

"It's Yule," Marissa explained. "She wanted to see the fireworks."

"Nevertheless—" Gwyn began to say. "In my day—"

I hurriedly cut her off. "We're so sorry we've disturbed you tonight."

"Under any other circumstances—"

"I want to go to meet the ghosts!" Gertie wailed. "Alfhild said I could."

"It's a long way," I told her. "We have to take a train and then drive in my old van."

"I don't care! I want to take a train!"

I began to move towards the front door, intent only on escape. Gertie's shrieking was approaching air raid-siren decibel levels. "I'll leave you to it," I told Marissa.

"I want to gooooooOOOO!" Gertie's face had turned purple.

Marissa clapped her hands over her ears. "Alright!" she said.

Gertie instantly quietened and rolled doe eyes at Marissa. "You mean it?" she asked. "Fank 'oo, Auntie Marissa."

I snuck a quick look at Gwyn, who had turned as pale as, erm, a ghost. I bared my teeth at her and she shuddered.

"Perhaps she'll sleep on the train," Marissa said.

"We can hope," I nodded, my fingers curling around the wand in my pocket. If she didn't, I might have to take drastic action.

Gertie did sleep on the train. So did Marissa. I tried and failed.

Instead, I drank my way through three bottles of water. By the time we alighted the train and reached the van in Bristol, I knew we'd have to stop for a bathroom break once we were on the motorway.

As it turned out, we stopped not just once but three times. And every time we parked up outside a neon automobile oasis, Gertie loudly and vociferously voiced her demands. To be fair, we had made a rod for our own backs by agreeing to bring her with us. Now she held us to ransom. If Marissa and I—Gwyn had elected to disappear soon after we left Tumble Town—didn't give in to her demands, this modern-day Veruca Salt threatened to scream the motorway services down. While it was fortunate that at this ridiculous time of the morning the services were quiet, this came hand in hand with the disadvantage that Gertie's pleas carried throughout the whole building.

Frankly, I was appalled by her behaviour, but still I gave in to her, furnishing her with comics, sweets and toys, all the while mainlining espresso like it was going out of fashion. Increased quantities of caffeine only added to my misery, and twenty minutes down the road we had to pull in again.

And on it went.

"Have you seen the price of these things?" I grumbled to Marissa as I purchased some peculiar green monster soft toy with memory foam insert and boggle eyes. "It's just overpriced tat."

"They certainly know what to charge," Marissa answered ruefully, clutching a handful of chocolate bars and a colouring book. We made it back to the van before realising we didn't have any colouring pencils or crayons, so Marissa had to be dispatched once more to purchase some of those.

No sooner were we underway again than my bladder seemed to fill of its own accord. I glared at the motorway signs. Could I really still be forty miles away from our final destination? I decided to practise some pelvic floor control. If we had to stop at yet another services, I would likely go bankrupt.

We arrived at the inn just after what would normally be six thirty in the morning. Of course, it wasn't. Time in Whittlecombe had not moved on at all. The same purple-grey twilight enshrouded the village, the icy drizzle covering everything in a sparkling layer that never seemed to get any deeper.

I couldn't remember a time when I'd felt so tired. The driving had taken it out of me. I led the way inside the inn, Gertie hopping energetically up the front steps behind me. I hoped against hope that everyone would be up and about, wondering where I'd been. Then I could look forward to sending Marissa and Gertie back to London with a heartfelt apology.

No such luck.

The large grandfather clock reminded me that it was still three fifty-eight in the afternoon. Archibald remained asleep at reception. In the bar, my guests were in the exact same positions I'd left them. I could smell roasting meats fragrancing the downstairs. Normally my stomach would have rumbled with desire, but now it rolled queasily. I glanced up the stairs. Everywhere remained eerily silent.

Gwyn apparated beside me. I glanced at her, hopeful that she had seen some of the other ghosts, but she only gave me a minute shake of the head and pressed her lips together.

Gertie banged the desk bell with the flat of her hand several times. Lucky for Archibald he was sound asleep, or he'd have been deafened. I gently moved it out of her reach.

"Can we see him?" Gertie asked.

"See who?" I queried, unsure whether she could see Archibald or not.

"Silvan. I want to see him."

"When he wakes up," Marissa told her, catching her hand.

"I want to see him now!"

"He's asleep," I reminded her. "He's not really in a fit state to see anyone."

"He'll see me," Gertie said, with the confidence of youth. "He likes me."

"Does he?" I shouldn't have sounded so doubtful, but this kid was a handful.

"Yes, he does!" By the scowl on Gertie's face, she was just about to kick off again.

"Why don't we get some breakfast?" I suggested. "Some bacon and egg or toast or ... something." It suddenly occurred to me that with all of Monsieur Emietter's pans on the go, I'd struggle to make anything more complicated than a bowl of cereal.

Gertie threw her head and shoulders forwards and rounded her back, making gagging noises. "I don't want breakfast! I feel sick!"

"Grand," I said.

Marissa grimaced. "Perhaps she could do with a proper sleep. Do you have a spare room?"

The inn was fully booked. There was my room, but Silvan was lying on the bed in there.

"Charity's room," I suggested. "I'll take you up there."

We led a protesting, whinging Gertie up the stairs to Charity's small but cosy box room on the second floor. The walls were whitewashed and plain, but there was an array of colourful rugs, throws and cushions to brighten the place up. As soon as Gertie lay down, her eyes closed and she went out like a light.

I breathed a sigh of relief.

"You look like you could do with a few hours' sleep yourself," Marissa whispered.

We pulled Gertie's door to, and I led Marissa down to the next level. We walked to my office. I didn't go inside; it felt wrong when Charity was asleep in there.

The Irish wolfhound had remained in situ outside the bedroom door. On seeing us, he pushed himself up, performed a downward dog followed by a back leg and neck stretch, yawned, shook himself, strolled away down the corridor and disappeared.

I watched him go. Oh, to be that relaxed. "I can't tell a lie," I said, "I'd kill for a nap."

"Well, why don't you have one?"

I hesitated. "It just seems wrong. I need to get to the bottom of what's going on and wake everyone up so we can all continue with our lives."

"You know, one of the things I've always admired about you, Alfhild, is how determined you are, and this ... this ... compunction you have to set the world to rights." Marissa folded her arms, smiling gently at me. "But you can't do it all. Not all at once. And not by yourself."

"But—"

"And if you make yourself ill, how is that going to be of any use to Silvan?"

I couldn't deny her logic. I stifled a yawn. "I tell you what," I said, "if you nip in there"—I indicated the door to my bedroom—"and kiss Silvan—"

Marissa frowned.

I held my hands up. "Look, I know what you're saying but as you've come all this way, you could at least try?"

"It won't make any difference."

"Kiss him," I begged. "Just the once. Then if nothing happens—and the goddess forbids it's still three fifty-eight—I'll have a sleep for a few hours, and we'll regroup after that."

"You make it sound like military manoeuvres," Marissa smirked, "but okay." She pointed at my bedroom door. "In here?"

I nodded.

"Do you want to come in?"

"Eww." I grimaced. "No thanks."

Marissa chuckled and gently opened the door. She peered inside. "Oh, Mr Hoo," she exclaimed. "He's asleep too. Do you want me to kiss him as well?"

"I don't think that's necessary," I said. Bad

enough she was kissing my beloved without kissing my familiar too.

She nodded and stepped inside. I pulled the door closed after her and retreated to a respectable distance, lining my back up against the wall as though facing a firing squad.

"Is everything alright, Alfhild?" Gwyn floated along the hallway towards me, back in her domain where she felt comfortable. The slinky whippet followed at her heels; the Irish wolfhound plodded more sedately behind them.

I nodded at my bedroom door. "Marissa's in there, doing the business."

"I think that's taking things a little too far, dear."

I blinked. "Grandmama! Not that kind of business. Just a kiss." I slumped and rocked my head back against the wall, hitting it a little harder than I'd intended. "Ow."

"Marissa's right, you could do with some sleep." Gwyn had been listening in to our conversation, then. Nothing ever remains private at Whittle Inn.

"I know, I know." I pointed at the whippet, who had settled on the floor close to Gwyn's feet, quite content. "Looks like you have a new friend."

"Hmpf." Gwyn stared down her nose at the poor

creature. "I have no idea why. I'm not encouraging the beast."

"Hardly a beast, is she?" I bent over to tickle her ears and she obligingly rolled over for a tummy rub. "Awww, you're a cutie!" I glanced up at my great-grandmother. "Maybe we should—"

"No," replied Gwyn, far too quickly. "Out of the question."

She was saved from further discussion on the matter of dog adoption by Marissa opening the door and stepping out into the hall.

I stood up to face her, half in dread, half in hope. "Any joy?"

Marissa shook her head. "Sorry, Alf. Not so much as a twitch."

"Hah!" I exhaled for a long time, allowing exhaustion and relief to flood through me. Marissa moved out of the door to give me a hug.

"There must be someone else," Gwyn was saying. I didn't want to think about that for now. Without saying anything else, I nodded at Marissa and moved into the bedroom.

Closing the door behind me, I threw off my cloak, yanked off my boots and collapsed onto the bed beside Silvan. Raising myself on one elbow, I stared down into his handsome face. "I don't care who you love the best," I told him, "I will find a way to wake you up anyway. We'll face the consequences afterwards."

With that, I lay my head on my pillow. Within moments, I'd joined him in slumberland.

Chapter Ten

It felt like only seconds later that I was awoken by rumbling and shrieking. Through habit, I glanced at my bedside clock.

Three fifty-eight.

Argh.

I rolled over. Silvan was in exactly the same position I'd left him. "If only there was some sort of time statute on this hex," I grumbled, sitting up and rubbing my eyes. Even the skin on my face felt tired. "Something that would take away the problem without me having to figure out what to do next."

I swung my legs over the side of the bed. "All I wanted was a party and a good time. Something nice to eat. A bit of a boogie ..."

I enjoyed a quick wallow in self-pity, all the while listening to the clunking and rumbling in the hall. It sounded as though the paintwork on my skirting board was taking a beating. I hoped that in Florence's absence, Gwyn wasn't trying to operate the vacuum.

In reality, I couldn't see that happening. My great-grandmother cleaning? Ha ha ha.

Reluctantly, I slithered over to the door, pulled it open and poked my head out. The Irish wolfhound had disappeared again; perhaps he'd gone to breakfast to escape the commotion. A trio of furry mutts chased past me. I leaned forward to see where they were going and spotted Gertie on an old tricycle, pedalling furiously down the hallway. When she reached the end—and the dogs had jumped up and licked her and barked and shaken and wagged their tails—she performed a nifty three-point turn, managing to clump into all three walls, and headed back towards me.

"Having fun?" I asked as she reached me.

She pulled up. "I went exploring," she said. "I found this in the attic."

"Fair enough." I decided that if a battered old bike kept her out of trouble, I could put up with a few scratched skirting boards. "It was probably my father's."

"Where is he?" she asked. "Is he dead?"

"More dead than alive," I said. "What about yours?"

"I don't have one," she said, matter-of-fact.

I nodded. "Yes, I know what that's like."

Gertie stared up at me. Her eyes were the same light blue as Marissa's. "Why?"

"He went away when I was young."

"Did you miss him?"

I crouched beside her, wondering where all the questions were leading. "I did. Very much so. But those we love are never lost to us."

"Did you get another daddy?"

"No." I shook my head, remembering my mother's grief. Her loneliness. It had sent her over the edge. "My mother never found anyone else."

"Would you have liked another daddy?"

I considered this for a moment. "Perhaps," I said. "But if I'm honest, it would probably have added to my mother's problems. She found it easier to be alone."

"Why?"

Because she was batpoop crazy, I wanted to say, but didn't. "Because my mother had certain challenges," I answered. I was being honest in that regard. "She ended up liking chickens more than people."

Gertie burst into laughter. It was the first time I'd seen her genuinely amused. I smiled too. It was a nice moment.

"Chickens?"

"Yes. I don't know why. But when she died, I had to find homes for dozens of them."

"I'd like a chicken."

"You'd need a chicken coop. Not sure what your Mum would think of that." I pointed at the dogs, who were waiting patiently for her to play with them again. "It looks like you have an affinity with animals."

"What's a finity?"

"Affinity. It means rapport, er, a natural liking. You get on with something or someone really well." I indicated the dogs again. "These guys like you."

"Do you think so?" Gertie looked pleased by this.

"My friend Millicent would say that dogs are a good judge of character. She would say if dogs are your friends, then that means you must be nice." I thought back to the devil-child I'd met the previous evening. She seemed like an entirely different character this morning.

"I'd like a dog."

"They need lots of exercise," I replied automatically. "I'm not sure Tumble Town is a good place for dogs."

"There are some parks," Gertie told me.

"Are there?" That surprised me. However, I'd been thinking less about exercising opportunities and more about some of the shady individuals in Tumble Town who might well appreciate dog on their supper menu.

"Yes." She reached out to stroke the fluffy white Jack Russell type thingummy hybrid. "I'd like a chicken and a dog and a daddy."

"Well, make the most of having these dogs to play with for now," I suggested. "I'm going to grab a shower. Then we should have something to eat. Are you hungry?"

"Always."

A child after my own heart.

Feeling a little more refreshed, I ventured downstairs twenty minutes later and went straight to the kitchen where Gwyn and Marissa were waiting for me.

Marissa was sitting at the kitchen table. "Gertie said she was hungry, but I wasn't sure what to do about cooking anything." She glanced around at the simmering pots. "This is a powerful magick that can hold time in such a way. Nothing is burning. It's remarkable."

I pulled open the oven door and regarded the contents. An enormous side of beef, roasting away with onions, and a massive piece of pork. Despite the fact that it had been cooking for what felt like days, nothing looked quite done yet. The only thing that was properly edible—unless I wanted to cook from scratch, and let's face it, Alf cooking is never a good idea—was the winter broth. I pulled out three soup bowls and ladled some into each, serving them up with some of Florence's crusty bread. Even that didn't have a hint of staleness.

Strange times.

Gertie screwed her face up. "Is this vegetable soup?"

Marissa opened her mouth to respond. I knew Marissa would tell the truth and we'd risk a meltdown and then I'd have to find sweets or crisps or ice cream instead—and I was absolutely convinced that part of Gertie's problem was too much sugar—so I jumped in quickly.

"Certainly not," I said. "What you have here"—I indicated my sleeping chef—"is Monsieur Emietter's finest top-secret recipe."

Gertie stirred her soup with distrust.

"Because he's a ghost," I explained, warming to my topic, "he has access to recipes from the realm beyond this one."

Gertie's eyes widened. "Beyond the veil?"

"Exactly!"

"But what's in it?" Gertie turned the corner of her lip up.

I tapped my nose and lowered my voice. "As I said, it's top secret ... but I did get a glance at his recipe book once and I'm pretty sure it said the tail of a griffin and the shank of a snake."

If Florence hadn't been slumbering somewhere, I'm certain I would have heard her exclaim, "Really, Miss Alf!" And if Monsieur Emietter had been awake and able to understand English, he would have thrown his cleaver at me.

"Ugh!" Gertie said, with feeling. "That sounds disgusting."

"It is," I admitted. "But the thing is ..." I lowered my voice even further so that Gertie had to lean closer to hear me. "Griffin and snake magick is powerful. A witch who eats this soup can only be stronger because of it." I supped a spoon of the broth and winked at her. "But don't tell anyone else, okay? It's our secret."

Gertie nodded and tucked in.

I resisted the urge to cheer when she asked for seconds.

"What's the plan now?" Marissa asked. We had remained at the kitchen table, in the warm, while Gertie had headed outside into the glum twilight, taking the dogs. She had gone in search of my ghost chickens. I poured coffee and considered stealing a slice of Florence's yule log, then decided against it. She would not be happy, when she woke up, to discover I'd cut into her festive masterpiece.

"There have to be other women in Silvan's life," Gwyn said, and not for the first time. I'd been trying not to listen because it wasn't something I wanted to consider.

Marissa hesitated. "I know of one other. Possibly two."

My stomach sank like a stone. "That's good. Could we get hold of them, do you think?"

"Hmmm. Now you're asking." Marissa thought for a moment. "We could check his phone."

I nodded. I hated to do it. It felt like prying into his most private self, but I knew he kept a great deal of information on his battered old Witchyberry. I'd once suggested I'd buy him a new one, a smarter, more up-to-date model, but he'd refused point-blank. He'd had the screen replaced on his old thing more times than I cared to remember.

"I think the time has come," I said and reluctantly made my way upstairs to find it. It was tucked into the inner pocket of his robes, pressed against his chest. I slid it out, warm from where it had nestled there, checked he was still comfortable and headed downstairs again. Only when I was in the presence of Marissa and my great-grandmother did I press the button and bring the phone to life. I'd feared I'd need a password or some code to get me into it, but he had nothing like that set up.

"No signal," I grumbled, waving the useless piece of junk I held in my hand at the others. I'd forgotten about my connectivity issues.

Marissa frowned and reached for it. "We could try and fix it," she said.

"How?" I yanked it away, ungenerously unwilling to share Silvan's private business with her.

Marissa's gentle smile was chastisement enough. "A little magick, perhaps?"

She flicked out a finger and, before I could

protest further, shot a thin silvery beam of energy at the device in my hand. "*Perfectus fluctus aeris!*"

The phone vibrated and, within seconds, I was alerted to eight new texts, four missed calls and twenty-three unread emails.

Marissa giggled with childish delight and I smiled too, a little grudgingly. Why hadn't I thought of that?

"Where do I start?" I held the phone up as it binged and bonged. Marissa twisted sideways to get a better look. "His girlfriend before you was called Venus. So let's try the contacts."

I nodded, pressed the wrong button a few times until I finally ended up where I needed to be. I scrolled through the list of names and numbers. Only one Venus. A Venus la Mística.

"La Mística?" I asked Marissa. "How very exotic."

Marissa nodded. "Italian," she said, by way of explanation.

I pressed my lips together. S*mashing*.

"Does it give any other details?" Gwyn asked. "Like how to find her?"

"Mmm. There's an address here. Oh." I sighed. "London. I could have killed two birds with one stone and brought her down last night."

"What if we let her know it's an emergency? Maybe she'll jump on a train?" Marissa suggested. "We could ask her?"

"What was she like?" I asked. "Would she be that accommodating, do you think?"

Marissa shrugged. "I, erm, maybe."

That didn't sound hopeful.

"What about the other woman?" I asked. I couldn't bring myself to call them Silvan's girlfriends.

"Delilah was delightful."

"Delilah?" I raised my eyebrows and began scrolling through the contacts again. "Delilah Greensoul."

"Hippy trippy but totally harmless." Marissa grinned at me.

"No surprise that with a name like that she lives in Glastonbury," I said. "Well, that's not a great distance. We can take a drive over there."

"How far does that take us back into Silvan's"—Gwyn coughed delicately—"history?"

Marissa shot me an apologetic smile. "Not all the way. There was another young woman, but I don't remember her name. He didn't talk about her a lot."

"Perhaps one of the other two will." I huffed out

my cheeks. "Do you actually know this Venus? Would she take a call from you?"

Marissa's eyes widened. "You want *me* to call her?"

I held up Silvan's phone. "Did they part on good terms? Would she answer a call from Silvan?"

"Very sneaky." Marissa nodded. "I'm not sure it was amicable but I think she would hear me out. We weren't bosom buddies but we rubbed along alright."

"Excellent." A sudden thought occurred to me. "Does anyone know what time it is in London?"

"I think it's around four in the afternoon," Gwyn said.

"Very funny, Grandmama." I scrunched my face up. *Three fifty-eight, no doubt.*

"I mean it, Alfhild. Around five to four in the real world."

"Has it only been twenty-four hours?" I refilled my coffee. "It feels a lot longer than that."

I quickly decided I was glad I'd suggested Marissa call Venus. I could only hear Marissa's side of the conversation, but it certainly sounded animated on the other end. Marissa had to use her finest powers of persuasion and her most soothing tone to calm the other woman down. When she finally thumbed the red button, she grimaced at me and let her breath out in a rush.

"She's still a dynamo," she said.

"What's the verdict? Will she come?"

"She's agreed to get on a train, yes. I said we'd pick her up from somewhere, so she'll text Silvan's phone once she's on her way."

"And she didn't mind?" I asked, slightly suspicious of her motives. I couldn't imagine what I would say if someone wanted me to go and kiss an ex-boyfriend.

"She says she has some unfinished business," Marissa shrugged.

"Probably a love child," Gwyn announced.

"Grandmama!"

"Well, I wouldn't put it past him," Gwyn said.

I shook my head, fairly certain he would have mentioned it if he had any children from previous relationships. "I don't know why you're being so mean about him. You and he get on very well." I pushed myself to my feet and drained my coffee. "Right. Let's hit the road."

"Are we all going?" Gwyn asked.

"Unless you want to stay here and babysit and dog sit?" I asked, hopefully.

"Absolutely not, Alfhild. My days of babysitting are long behind me."

"Then yes, we're all going," I said.

CHAPTER ELEVEN

While Marissa prised Gertie away from the ghost chickens, I used Silvan's phone to call Delilah. Mine refused to work, no matter what Marissa tried to do to it. A rather laidback message on the answerphone, with a snuffly voice that reminded me of Perdita Pugh, informed me that Delilah couldn't take my call but she looked forward to reaching out to me shortly.

I hung up and then instantly tried again, impatient to get hold of her. Without success. I decided to kerb my impatience. It wasn't a good look, being desperate enough to leave several dozen messages in a row on someone's voicemail.

The next issue I had was how to travel back from Glastonbury with Delilah, Marissa, Gertie and possibly Venus in the van? The van had two front seats and space in the back with a hard floor. We'd managed on the way back from Bristol because Gertie had been sitting in the front and Marissa wasn't one to complain, but that would never do once we had Delilah in tow.

I solved the problem by gathering up several armfuls of cushions, along with a pair of single mattresses we kept for put-me-ups or shake-you-downs or whatever they were called—temporary beds in guest rooms, anyway—and arranging those in the back of the van, until effectively what I had in there was a huge squashy bed. It looked quite cosy. I could have happily climbed in and bedded down for the night.

"Are we taking a picnic?"

I reversed, backside first, out of the rear of the van. Gertie was standing watching me, one of the small fluffier dogs by her side. She had it on a lead, I noted.

"We've only just eaten," I reminded her. She had an appetite that was even healthier than mine.

"The picnic's for later," she pointed out.

"I'll ask Fl—" I started to say, but I couldn't ask Florence. I'd have to concoct something myself from Monsieur Emietter's nibbles and pastries, put aside for the party. "I'll find something," I promised. I pointed at the dog. "You can let him free inside the inn. He won't need to be on his lead."

"His name is Sampson."

"That's a big name for a little dog."

"He wants to come with us."

"No he doesn't," I said, frowning down at the dog. "You don't, do you?" I suddenly had an awful feeling he might answer me, like a canine version of Wizard Magigi, so I hurried on before he could interrupt me. "You see, the thing is, Gertie, dogs like to have a lot of sleep and … erm … they get carsick a lot." I had no idea whether that was true, but it sounded plausible.

"It's not a car, it's a van."

"Van sick, then." I motioned towards the inn. "Let's go and get that picnic, and we can find somewhere for, ah, Sampson here to relax while we're gone. What do you say?"

"He's hungry."

"He can't be," I protested. "I fed him yesterday!"

"Didn't you know dogs have to be fed every day, Alf?" Gertie was asking me for about the twentieth time. She found my lapse hilarious.

I glanced at her through the rear-view mirror. She was sucking on a lollipop and cuddling Sampson. We had hardly even managed to get out of Whittlecombe yet, and I was already wishing I could have left everyone else at the inn.

We'd had to stop off at Whittle Stores so that I could buy more dog food and treats—at the last count there were thirty-two spoiled pooches inhabiting Whittle Inn, settling on every soft surface the inn possessed, although I'd drawn the line at the guests' beds.

Or rather, Gwyn had. We had to maintain standards, she told me.

Where they had all come from, I had no idea. They just kept turning up.

While in the shop, Gertie had collected together an enormous bagful of sweets and snacks. Marissa, being Marissa, and quite possibly the most permissive aunt I'd ever met, had allowed her niece to 'buy' the goodies. It had been me who had coughed up the cash, of course. I left another thirty pounds behind the till, aware that I'd now wiped Whittle Stores out of almost all its dog food.

If I didn't wake everyone up soon, I'd have to feed the dogs cat food, and then where would we be, I wondered.

What might the side effects be?

Dogs who meowed? Who refused to come when called?

I had to stop just outside of Honiton to put some petrol in the tank. For the first time since we'd left the inn, I began to see other cars, and the light icy rain that had been falling relentlessly on Whittlecombe for what felt like a million years finally dried up. I was glad of that. The sleet made the roads slippery, and I was already a little worried about the van's performance.

The engine didn't sound too healthy. We'd probably been lucky to get to and from Bristol in the old thing.

After I'd filled it up, I gave the windscreen a quick clean and pulled my wand out from the pocket of my robes. I paused, unsure what kind of magick I could use on a car. What I really needed was help from a mechanical wizard, but I didn't know any. Reluctantly, I stuffed the wand back in my pocket. It really wouldn't do to ask the van to fix itself, just in case I did something and couldn't undo it. I considered asking it to 'hang on', but even that might be misconstrued. In this part of East Devon, I was liable to find myself teetering over the edge of a cliff in the van, with Gertie jumping up and down on the bumper, shouting 'fly free' at me.

No, no. I'd leave it for now.

"How far is it now?" Gertie asked as I climbed inside and started the engine.

"It's a long way yet," I warned her. "So it's probably best if you and Sampson snuggle up and have a kip."

"I'm not tired." Gertie dismissed my suggestion and reached for a Sherbet Dib Dab.

"Alright," I said, swapping a glance with Marissa sitting next to me. She shrugged.

I turned the radio on. Mariah Carey's dulcet tones blasted out. All she wanted for Christmas, apparently, was you.

Baby.

"Do turn that down, Alfhild. I can hardly hear myself think above that hideous wailing."

"Is it necessary for you to think, Grandmama?" I muttered under my breath.

"I heard that, my dear. Of course I need to think! We can't leave everything to you."

It was going to be a long trip.

The traffic grew heavier once we were on the M5 heading north. Perhaps I should have taken the back roads rather than the motorway, but I wasn't entirely sure of the way and didn't want to risk the van on slippery mud-covered roads and narrow lanes in the dark. But of course, anyone with half a brain would have known that the major routes would be busy.

Because unfortunately, *I* hadn't factored in Christmas.

It seemed that the entire population of the West Country was heading somewhere else. To Wales, to Heathrow and London, to Birmingham and the Midlands; anywhere except around the corner. For over an hour I hardly managed to get out of second gear. The van juddered and coughed, sounding increasingly exhausted—a bit like me—but at least it managed to keep going.

I glared at the red taillights in front of us, my head beginning to ache. Mercifully, for my sanity at least, Gwyn had retreated to wherever it was she went when she wasn't in the mood to deal with life, love and the universe—or people—but that still left Gertie. And the more sugar that Gertie consumed, the louder and crankier she became.

"You know," I tried, when all other avenues of calming her down had failed, "if you keep this up,

Father Christmas is going to think twice about coming to see you in a few days."

"Father Christmas?" Gertie sneered. "We don't have Christmas in our house. Mummy says it's all made up."

I looked sideways at Marissa. She nodded. "My family have never gone in for it."

My mouth dropped open. "Ever?"

Marissa shook her head. "I don't think I've ever celebrated anything except Yule."

Gertie slapped me on the back of the head. It was a good job I had so much hair, it protected me from such an onslaught. It still hurt though. "Mummy says it's just a story, made up by capitalists."

I snorted. "If that's so, how come I've met him?"

"You haven't met him. You're fibbing." Gertie sounded very sure of herself.

"I have too," I told her. "Last year, in fact."

"I don't believe you." Gertie hit me on the head again.

"Ow." I bit my tongue to stop myself from remonstrating with her.

Marissa turned around. "Gertie, that isn't nice."

"I don't care."

"Fine," I retorted, at the end of my tether. "You

sound like someone who doesn't care about *anything* very much. That's not an especially good way to live your life, but you go for it!"

Marissa placed a gentle hand on my thigh. "To be fair, she is only six."

"Well, yes," I growled, "but I'm fairly sure I cared about lots of things by the time I was six."

"Like what?" Marissa asked.

"Like trees and animals and … and … Father Christmas!"

"Not world peace, then?" Marissa smiled.

Her gentle jibe took the heat out of the situation. "No, I think I waited until I was seven to care about world peace," I admitted. "And I was eight before I bought my first CND and Greenpeace badges. I pinned them to my school bag."

We remained silent for a while. In Gwyn's absence I'd turned the radio back on. Chrissie Hynde was warbling about how far two thousand miles was. I understood her pain. I felt like I'd travelled at least that distance, but in actual fact, we'd only managed forty miles.

The phone in Marissa's lap pinged. "It's Venus," she told me. "She's on the train. Where can we pick her up?"

I did a quick calculation of where we were in

relation to the mainline stations. "I tell you what, ask her to get off at Taunton. We can meet her there. And tell her to wait. We might be late given how long it's taking us just to do the first part of the journey." I slapped the steering wheel in frustration.

Marissa texted back and a few moments later the phone pinged again. "She says okay."

"Jolly good."

Gertie had fallen quiet and I'd hardly noticed, but the temporary peace was shattered when she smacked me on the head again.

"Were you fibbing when you said you met Father Christmas?" she asked.

"Well, I didn't exactly meet him—"

"I knew it!" Gertie sounded triumphant.

"But close enough. I found one of his reindeer in Speckled Wood and he flew over Whittle Inn and collected him. He left me a present."

"What was he like?" Gertie wanted to know. I stole a look in the rear-view mirror. Her eyes were wide.

"He seemed like a genuinely nice man. A jolly man."

"Was he fat? I've seen pictures. He looks fat."

"Quite chubby. In a cuddly way. He obviously enjoys cake. And sweets."

"I like sweets."

No kidding. "A very decent man. Who *cares* about things."

"What does he care about?"

"Other people's happiness," I told her. "He likes to make people smile. I think that's a really lovely goal to have in life. Don't you?"

"I don't know."

"Put it this way," I said. "When you're happy, how does that feel inside?"

Gertie considered this quite seriously. "It makes me feel like I have bubbles in my tummy and that my heart is smiling."

"And wouldn't it be nice to make other people feel that way?"

Gertie thought some more. "Yes," she said finally. "I suppose so."

"Well, I think that's what Father Christmas aims to do. And it's nice. He makes everyone feel happy, and when we're happy it's easier to spread happiness around."

"So did you feel happy when you met him?"

I thought back to my encounter with Father Christmas outside Whittle Inn. It gave me a warm and fuzzy feeling. "Yes. I did."

"And he gave you a present?"

"A marvellous present." My heart fluttered at the memory.

"I'd like a present."

I smiled. It seemed a shame that she wouldn't celebrate Christmas and have any gifts. "If you're a good girl for the rest of the journey, maybe I'll put in a good word for you and Father Christmas will bring you a present that you can open on Christmas morning."

Gertie squealed. "And one for Sampson?"

What had I started?

"Don't forget Sampson isn't yours," I reminded her. "He'll need to go back to his owner when we've sorted everything out."

"No! He loves me!" Her voice began to rise.

Uh-oh.

"Gertie, you know we can't take a dog home," Marissa interjected.

Gertie began to wail. "I want to!"

"That's impossible," Marissa replied, her voice kind but firm.

Gertie set about wailing like a banshee. I cringed.

Fortuitously, the traffic ahead of me suddenly freed up and I was able to slip into third gear and start to move forwards at speed. The county boundary sign reading Somerset was a ray of sunshine on a bleak horizon. Wham were singing about last Christmas and giving away their innards, and all I wanted to do was locate a cave in Speckled Wood and hide away until Gertie had headed home with Marissa.

The things we do for love, eh?

Especially when that love is, apparently, not being reciprocated.

Who was Silvan's true love?

It was time to find out.

CHAPTER TWELVE

Delilah Greensoul.

Marissa had described her as delightful, and I suppose in her own completely potty way, she was. I, for one, absolutely could not see her in a relationship with Silvan at all. Slightly older than he, she was one of those wonderful witches who preferred everything in life to be *au naturel*. Rather like Frau Krauss, who roamed the forests all day long, or Tempestas Darkskull, a member of Kappa Sigma Granma whom I'd met earlier this year and who liked to parade around in the altogether, Delilah was a majestic free spirit.

She lived in a ramshackle cottage—actually more of a rundown bungalow—on the edge of Glastonbury, not a million miles away from the famous tor. Ivy climbed the external walls, cracking and dislodging the pebbledash cladding, and the paint on the window frames was peeling away. What it did have going for it was a large amount of outside space and, while at this time of year it was difficult to tell, it did appear that Delilah was green-fingered. During the spring and summer, her garden would be an oasis of flora and fauna.

I held down the bell push for longer than was strictly necessary until the door was gently pulled open and a fortyish-year-old woman peered out at me. Her frizzy hair, a dull chestnut colour but with more than her fair share of greys, was caught up in an untidy bun. "Hello," she said. She cocked her head to stare at the van on the road outside. Pine needles and bits of dead leaf fell from her hair. Her face was streaked green, as though she had been nuzzling a damp tree trunk recently and had forgotten to look in a mirror.

"Delilah Greensoul?" I decided I'd better check before I made any more assumptions.

"Ye-es." She sounded unsure, looking me up and down.

"Hi. I've been trying to get hold of you," I told her. "We've been calling and texting you."

She smiled uncertainly. "Oh dear, have you?"

"I'm Alfhild Daemonne." I waited to see whether there was any flicker of recognition but there was none. If Silvan had been in touch with her at all lately, he hadn't told her about me. "I've travelled up from Whittle Inn in Whittlecombe, East Devon. I'm —" I hesitated but, in the end, I needed her to know the facts. "I'm Silvan's girlfriend."

Now she looked surprised. "That's a blast from the past," she said. Her brow creased. "He's not hurt, is he? Not—?"

"No," I infilled hurriedly. "He's okay. Kind of. But I do need your help."

"Did you want to come in?" She pulled the door open. She was wearing little more than a sheer silk shift. It didn't leave a lot to the imagination. A black cat curled around her feet, and I could see a few more behind her, staring at me as quizzically as their mistress.

"That would be marvellous. I'm not alone, though." I pointed in the direction of the van. "I have my friend Marissa with me. You probably remember her. And her niece, Gertie."

"Marissa?" Delilah relaxed. "Oh, I do remember her! A lovely, lovely lady! Bring them in. I'll find a robe."

We settled down in Delilah's cosy living room and accepted her kind offer of tea. Gertie slumped on a huge armchair, in a sulk because I'd insisted she leave Sampson in the van, in deference to Delilah's cats. Delilah tempted the child's good humour by offering biscuits from a festive selection box and I grimaced inwardly as Gertie began knocking them back.

As Marissa and Delilah exchanged pleasantries, I looked around the room with interest. The furniture was old but well nurtured, the three-piece suite covered in colourful throws. Delilah had installed a small altar in the corner of the room. Candles burned amid pinecones and acorns and a selection of autumn leaves. Plants had been positioned everywhere: bushes and climbers and trailing things, fruit trees and a few poinsettias. The very air in the room was alive with the vibrancy of plant life. My headache faded and I felt somehow renewed.

Delilah had a number of caged birds. Or rather she had birds, all with the most beautiful plumage: a parakeet, a pair of parrots, several canaries and a couple of budgerigars, but the cage doors all stood resolutely open and the birds were free to go where they wished. The black cat I'd spotted earlier waited for Delilah to take her seat and then made itself comfortable in her lap, oblivious to the birds and to Gertie trying to cajole kitty away from his mistress.

"You said you needed my help?" Delilah offered

me the tray of biscuits and I took a couple of digestives. Gertie had swiped all the fancy cream and chocolate ones. I took a bite of one and winced. Stale. Perhaps they were out of date. They weren't a patch on Florence's homemade biccies.

I missed her.

"We do," Marissa said and nodded at me. "Alf?"

I explained the circumstances to Delilah. She sat and listened with rapt attention, as wide-eyed at my story as Gertie had been when I'd told her about meeting Father Christmas.

"Intense!" she exclaimed. "But what is it you think I can do, exactly?"

"We believe the hex can be broken with a kiss. But it has to be a true love's kiss."

Gertie yawned loudly.

Marissa reached for her. "Please cover your mouth when you yawn," she reminded her niece.

"Kissing is icky," Gertie reminded us.

"Hush, darling," Marissa said.

Delilah smiled at Gertie and turned to me. "I'm flattered, but I really don't think I could be described as Silvan's true love."

Now that I'd met her in the flesh, as lovely as she was, I couldn't see it myself either. She was such a soft, gentle person, rather like Marissa but much less ethereal. I imagined that Delilah would be no match for him. Not enough of a challenge.

Was I a challenge?

Perhaps I was too much of a challenge. Maybe that's why I wasn't his true love, either.

"Could you at least try?" I asked. "I know it's short notice, but we can take you to the inn and then I'll drive you home again." The thought of repeating the whole journey did not fill me with unconfined joy, but what's a lovesick witch to do?

Delilah shrugged and glanced at Marissa. "I'm happy to."

"Thank you." I breathed a sigh of relief.

"Silvan and I had a wonderful relationship," Delilah told me. "Mainly because we didn't bother each other. It was a no-pressure fling that should have probably lasted a matter of weeks, if that. In the end, we were together for a couple of years. Nearer five actually. We muddled along."

It didn't sound like a promising relationship, the way she talked about it.

"I think he'd had his heart broken before he found me—"

I perked my ears up.

"And that's why he settled for what I offered. Which wasn't a lot." Her eyes lost focus as she drifted into her memories. "I'm a free spirit. I didn't want commitment. I never have. I never will."

"And you think he does?" I couldn't see that myself. I knew—or I'd imagined I knew—that he and I belonged to each other, but what form that took I had no idea. And now it turned out that his heart belonged to someone else.

Venus?

Or what about this other woman Delilah was referring to?

"Do you happen to know who the person was who broke his heart?" I asked. She sounded promising.

"Ooh, now you're asking." Delilah leaned back and rolled her head up to stare at the ceiling. One of the parakeets flew across the room, landed on the back of her chair and rummaged in her hair.

I didn't want to know what she had living in that bird's nest of a hairdo.

"It was a long time ago, but I know she lived in a toll house not far from Lyme Regis."

I sat up a little straighter. This sounded like an interesting lead. "When you say a long time ago, how long are we talking?" I did a few swift calculations in my head. He and I had been 'together', whatever that turned out to mean, for around eighteen months.

Possibly he and Marissa had had a thing. Before that he'd been with Venus, and Marissa thought they'd been together for six months or so. It's impossible to weight a relationship based only on the amount of time people are together—I understood that—but between the four of us and the mysterious heartbreaker, we had surely dialled down into the nitty-gritty of Silvan's romantic past.

"Did he talk to you about her?" I wanted to know, anxious for any clues.

"Minimally and grudgingly," Delilah replied, plucking the bird from her head where it was trying to nest. "But I saw the way he looked at that house whenever we passed it and I asked him about it once. He said something like it had once been the loci for his hopes but was now the receptacle of his pain."

"How very poetic." I raised an eyebrow.

"I thought so." Delilah failed to notice my sarcasm.

"There would be no harm in driving over there and enquiring," Marissa suggested.

I had to concur. Nothing ventured, nothing gained. "It'll be a surprise for him after all these years," I noted and began mentally plotting a route. "We'll nip over to Taunton first and pick up Venus." It wouldn't be 'nipping' exactly, but as these things go it wasn't too ridiculously far away. "Then we'll go home via Lyme. Can you navigate us to this place?"

Delilah nodded. "Oh, yes. No trouble at all. It's a bit of a landmark. And I've been in the habit of thinking of Silvan every time I've passed it over the years. It's funny how people get under your skin that way, isn't it?"

"It really is," I said.

Chapter Thirteen

"How did you and Silvan meet?" I asked Delilah.

We were parked outside the railway station in Taunton, waiting for the 'fast' train from London Paddington to arrive. True to form, it was running slow and was therefore late.

"I run workshops," she replied simply. When I opened my mouth to ask the most obvious follow-up question, she sighed as though it was a terrible nuisance to answer. I kept schtum, but she took pity on me anyway and filled in the blanks.

"I'm a therapist. I do past life regression."

"Did Silvan come to you wanting to know about his past life?" I asked, genuinely shocked at the notion.

"Goodness me, no. I'd been asked to run some

sessions up and down the country—by the Ministry of Witches, in fact. He turned up to one in Tumble Town. By mistake, he always claimed, but I'm not sure I ever believed him." She gave me a knowing look. "I think he might have been following someone in my group."

That did sound more like Silvan.

"I invited my students for a drink afterwards. I always think it's nice to decompress. The workshops can be a little emotional. Silvan came along and we hit it off."

"Nice," I said, because I was unsure what the correct etiquette was for holding a conversation about how your boyfriend met his ex.

"What's past life transgression?" Gertie wanted to know.

"Regression," Marissa corrected her, although past life transgression would have fitted Silvan to a T.

"*Re*gression," Gertie repeated. "What is it?"

Delilah ran a hand through her hair, sprinkling herself and the passenger seat area with forest debris. "It's a therapy that helps people look back at their past lives. Sometimes we even look into someone's present life at their deeply buried memories."

"Oh." Gertie sounded disinterested. "It helps you remember things?"

"Yes," Delilah said.

"Mummy just makes lists," Gertie said. I hid my smile.

"Where is your mummy?" Delilah wanted to know. I'd been wondering that too, but hadn't liked to ask.

"She's away. With Honchez." Gertie almost spat the words.

I wiggled round in my seat to look first at her and then at Marissa. Marissa looked a little uncomfortable. *Who is Honchez?* I mouthed.

Mother's boyfriend, she mouthed back.

Ah. Gertie didn't like Honchez. You didn't have to be a therapist to see what was going on here. Of course, Gertie was feeling put out and neglected. Her mother had headed off over Yule with her new boyfriend and left her with Marissa. No wonder the little girl was tetchy and antagonistic. She felt abandoned.

"Don't you like H—" Delilah started to ask Gertie.

I reached over and brushed something off her chest. "I think that was alive," I said.

Instantly distracted, Delilah began to search for

whatever it had been and forgot about quizzing Gertie any further. "You were a bit rough there. I hope you haven't killed it, Alf," she scolded.

"It may not have been alive," I said hurriedly. "It may just have been leaf mould."

"Can you put the light on?" Delilah asked, and I could hear the rising tide of anxiety in her voice. Fortunately for me, through the nearby railings, I spotted movement. A large and noisy train had picked the perfect moment to arrive.

"This must be it!" I said, hopping out of the van before anyone could stop me. We'd sent a text to Venus to let her know we'd be waiting for her near the taxi rank. People streamed off the train, heavily laden with suitcases and bags full of gifts, many wrapped in tinsel or wearing festive hats, sparkly earrings and fashion brooches. I waited for the masses to disperse and for waiting families to grab their nearest and dearest and then made a beeline for the one young woman who stood alone.

Probably about my age, there the resemblance ended. She turned as I approached her, and I found myself in awe of her spectacular good looks. Definitely of Mediterranean heritage, she had long dark hair caught up in two thin ponytails, thick eyelashes framing brown eyes, and a perfect mouth, with lips neither too swollen nor too thin. She was as tall and thin as a supermodel, bordering on gangly, but carrying it off effortlessly. She stood even taller in six-inch-high sparkling stilettos, her torso wrapped in an imitation Yak-skin bomber jacket—that would have made me look like the back end of a double-decker bus—over leather trousers that appeared to have been spray-painted on. She clutched the handle of a small compact suitcase on wheels and glared into the shadows.

I must admit I was slightly taken aback by Venus. Apparently, Silvan didn't have a 'type'? How had he gone from Delilah—all hippy trippy bonkerness—to Venus and on to me? Although I suppose we had to factor Marissa into the equation too, didn't we? No matter what she said. She had more in common with Venus than Delilah and I did.

Harrumph.

In fact, the only thing each of us had in common, as far as I could tell, was notable hair. So maybe Silvan had a thing for hair.

"Venus?" I asked and held my hand out.

After a beat, she took it in her own kid-leather gloved one and gave me a single shake.

"I'm Alfhild Daemonne," I told her, "but you can

call me Alf if you like. Thanks so much for coming down here at such short notice."

"You're the current squeeze, are you?" she asked. Even her accent sounded exotic. Hot and fiery and passionate, the letters rolling from her tongue to lengthen the words. The look she gave me clearly indicated she thought Silvan's taste had declined in the time she and he had been apart.

"Yes," I said, trying not to bristle. She'd come a long way after all. "You must be tired."

"I'm totally exhausted. If I'd known the train would end up running so late, I would never have bothered. And it didn't even have a buffet car!"

I sympathised. It was probably the same train I'd been on … yesterday? Today? Earlier? What time zone was I in?

"I'm sorry about that. I'll make sure you get something decent to eat when we get back to the inn."

"Is it like a bed and breakfast that you run?" she asked, with such a tone of contempt that I quite withered inside.

"No, it's a proper country inn," I told her, "with bedrooms over several floors."

She sniffed. "Sounds lush."

"It is," I replied, firmly closing off all doubt. "The

van's over here." I pointed at Jed's van. Delilah was staring out of the passenger window at us, waving the fingers of her left hand in an eccentric greeting. I could see Gertie, staring open-mouthed, over her shoulder.

"*That* van?" Venus's voice rose in horror.

"I'm afraid so. I don't have access to any other transport."

"Couldn't you have hired a car or a taxi or something? Made an effort?"

"It's more comfortable than it looks, I promise."

Venus curled her lip and thrust her wheelie suitcase at me. "Take this. I'll have to sit in the front. I get carsick in the back."

I wheeled the suitcase across the road and opened the passenger door. "Sorry, Delilah. Would you be a darling, my love, and sit in the back with Marissa and Gertie?" I didn't mention Sampson the dog, but I was sure Delilah wouldn't be averse to a little dog hair. She loved all creatures, after all.

"Oh. Alright." Delilah looked slightly taken aback but jumped out readily enough. "By the way, Alf, I had a good look on the floor, but I don't think you killed anything." She patted my arm as she moved past me to open the back doors.

I indicated the empty seat to Venus, who had

followed me at a distance. She tip-tapped closer on her impossible heels, wobbling on the uneven road. When she bent over and scrutinised the pine needles and dried leaves, the dead grass, bird feathers and the insect cases with evident disgust, I hurriedly swept the seat clean.

"We have to make one more stop," I told her, hoping she would move a little faster. "It shouldn't take long ..."

While Venus settled herself into the front and reacquainted herself with Marissa—thank goodness for Marissa's patience and friendliness—I helped Delilah into the back, thrust the suitcase in after her, and slammed the door.

"Has everyone been introduced?" I asked as I buckled myself into the driver's seat. There were murmurs to the affirmative.

Uttering a little prayer to the goddess of automation, and another to the goddess of fortitude, I started the van's engine. It coughed and spluttered and came to life.

Thank you, thank you, thank you!

"I need to go." Gertie's dulcet tones rang out in the silent van.

I'd tried to make a little small talk as we drove, but Venus had remained monosyllabic and Delilah appeared to have lapsed into a trance. Only Marissa showed any interest, but given how much time we'd spent in each other's company over the past however many hours it had been, we didn't really have a lot to say to each other.

Nothing new anyway.

We were ten minutes down the road from Taunton railway station. "Go where?" I asked stupidly.

"You know!" Gertie howled at me, clearly imagining I was both dense and deaf.

"To the bathroom?" Venus suggested, delicately shielding her ears with her hands.

"Yes. Obvs!" Gertie hit me on the back of the head.

"Ow!" I took a deep breath. "Alright. "Everyone keep your eyes peeled. Maybe we'll find services or a café or something." I doubted it though. We were well off the beaten track now, dropping down from the M5, driving along unlit back roads, heading directly south for the coast. We were unlikely to find services, and most cafés were closed at this time of night. The best we might hope for was a petrol station.

"I need to go NOW!"

"Alright, alright!" I uttered a new prayer, this one to the goddess of comfort breaks and, as luck would have it, about a mile outside of Lyme Regis, on a dark, tree-lined B-road, we came across a petrol station lit up like a beacon. It was one of those tiny ones with a spotty teenager behind the glass at one end nursing the till, while the rest of the shop was lined with shelves displaying overpriced bagged sweets, crisps in every flavour known to witchkind, newspapers that surely no-one ever buys, car air fresheners, small containers of engine oil, meat pies, sandwiches, pork pies and nearly-out-of-date pasties.

The illuminated sign on the way onto the forecourt showed the universally recognised symbol for lavatories, along with a knife and fork.

"Hurry! Hurry!" begged Gertie, and I threw open my door and raced around the back of the van to let her out.

Marissa clambered out first. "I'll take her. I might as well use the facilities while we're here."

"Me too, in that case," Delilah said, so I helped her out too.

Venus was opening her door.

"Are you—?" I pointed a thumb in the direction of the rundown building behind me.

She wrinkled her nose. "No no. These places are always so unsavoury. I could kill for a decent coffee though."

At this petrol station? She would be sadly disappointed, I felt. "Me too. I'll go in and see what they have if you stay with the van?"

"No problem." She stretched and yawned. I slammed the van door and followed the others inside.

It turned out that there was a single bathroom in this particular petrol station that had to serve both staff and customers. Delilah and Marissa were queuing outside, both looking travel-weary and pale, and not entirely thrilled at the prospect of patronising these facilities.

I decided against joining them and, after perusing the shelves of Christmas 'gift' ideas—hand-wound torches, solar lights for your patio, mass-produced soft toys wearing Santa hats, toilet paper with crosswords printed on it and cheap chocolate bars shaped like snowmen—I located the coffee machine. As someone who had fresh tea and coffee on tap all day, every day, thanks to Florence, I couldn't help but stare with dismay at the branded vending machine. I might have been tempted to forego a coffee for my own part, but I'd promised Venus I'd bring her one back, so I rummaged in my purse for the change I needed and began the process.

As I waited for the second cup to fill, Gertie joined me with a handful of sweets. "Can I get a hot chocolate?" she asked.

"May I," I corrected her.

"May you what?"

"May I have a hot chocolate."

"And me. I want one." Gertie held her hands up. "Can you get these as well?"

"Where are your manners?" I asked.

"Please," she groaned. "Please can you get these?"

"Haven't you had enough? I'd hate you to be ill." I would. I would *really* hate her to throw up in the back of the van, especially with the mattresses and all the cushions in there. I'd bet good money that Marissa and Delilah wouldn't be best pleased either.

Fortunately, Marissa arrived at that moment—surreptitiously wiping her hands on the back of her robe, which told me everything I needed to know about her bathroom experience—and saved me from an argument with Gertie. I nodded at the goodies in Gertie's hands and left them to it. I was rapidly running out of willpower where it came to helping Marissa with her little niece.

I carried my coffees over to the young man at the till. He regarded us with a degree of curiosity. I suppose we did look a sight: me in my long black hooded cloak; Marissa and Delilah in robes; and Delilah shedding pine needles and bits of dried leaf everywhere she turned. Added to which, Gertie was now having a meltdown. The noise was deafening in such a confined space.

I stole a glance back at the three of them. "There, there," Delilah soothed.

Marissa shot a helpless glance my way. "Sorry," she said, "I didn't bring my purse."

She was going to give in to Gertie again? Heavens. But when Gertie's wails threatened to make my eardrums explode, I relented. "Alright. I'll buy them." I was in danger of becoming as lenient as Marissa was.

Gertie jabbed at the buttons on the vending machine and I dashed over before she could break it. I organised a hot chocolate, took her sweets from her and paid for everything on my card.

"Any petrol?" the young man asked.

I shook my head. I would be left penniless at this rate.

"Everyone back in the van," I ordered, grabbing my receipt. We trooped outside into the neon-lit darkness, the cashier watching us every step of the way. "The 'lovely' Venus will think we've deserted her."

Or maybe she'd be pleased if we did.

CHAPTER FOURTEEN

We passed a sign that proclaimed, *Welcome to Lyme Regis, Ancient Royal Borough, Gateway to the Jurassic Coast.*

Nearly there.

I flipped on the windscreen wipers. The closer we came to East Devon, the more the weather seemed to deteriorate. It was raining here. I'd hazard a guess that by the time we made it as far as Honiton, the sleet would be back. We were pulling uphill now, the engine whining a little. I put that down to having rather a lot of unaccustomed weight on board.

Delilah was leaning forwards, peering over my shoulder, ready to direct me as soon as she spotted something she recognised.

"So why are we going to Lyme Regis?" Venus asked. We'd been travelling along in silence for a few miles, which in some ways had been blissful for me, but in other ways strangely unnerving. Venus had a formidable energy, the type that can silence even the brightest of gatherings. However, I sensed beneath her bored tone a genuine interest in the answer.

"Delilah remembers that Silvan had a girlfriend prior to her. I want to see if I can track her down and persuade her to come with us. If I do, then we'll have dotted all the i's and crossed the t's. It's on the way back to the inn anyway, so it's not much of a detour."

"A girlfriend from before Delilah?" Venus asked.

"Yes. I know it's a long shot that she'll still be here," I admitted. "She might even be married with children by now; it was quite a while ago—"

Venus made a small noise in her throat.

"What?" I asked, my toes curling. She knew something.

"She's dead."

I was so surprised I hit the brakes. The van skidded to a stop.

"There it is!" Delilah shouted. We'd pulled up on the crest of a hill, my headlights picking out a small, round house at the corner of the junction. A typical old toll house, standing by itself on the road to the town.

"How do you know she's dead?" I frowned at Venus.

"Who's dead?" Delilah asked.

"Has someone died?" Gertie wanted to know. "Did you hit someone, Alf? Is that why we've stopped?"

"Ssssh," Marissa urged her niece. "Alf's a good driver."

Well, that at least was good to know. "Everything is fine," I told Gertie.

"You'd say that anyway," Gertie grumbled. "You all treat me like a baby."

"That's because you behave like one," said Venus, with the voice of a woman on the edge.

I darted a slightly concerned glance her way. She glared at me in return.

"I do not!" moaned Gertie. "Tell them I don't, Marissa. Tell them!"

Sampson whined.

"Is there a dog in here?" Venus asked. "I don't like dogs." Thank goodness Gwyn was elsewhere. Between her and Venus, they'd have abandoned poor Sampson in a nearby field.

Something dazzled me in the rear-view mirror, a car coming up behind us. I quickly threw the van into the correct gear, performed a slightly accelerator-heavy hill start and continued to the crossroads ahead. After crossing it safely, I drove a little way down the hill and pulled in to let the car behind us pass. I parked up, the toll house just behind us on our left.

"She won't be there because she's dead," Venus reminded me as though I hadn't heard the news the first time.

"How do *you* know?" Delilah asked in surprise. "He never told me that."

"Nor me," said Marissa.

Nor me, I added silently. But then I had no idea about Delilah or Venus either.

"Well he *did* tell me," Venus growled. She flipped off her seatbelt and flung open her door. "I need some air. It's cloying in here." She slipped out into the rain and disappeared to the rear.

I stared through the windshield, chewing on the inside of my cheek, watching the wipers go back and forth, back and forth. I suppose in the grand scheme of things it didn't matter that Silvan's first girlfriend was dead. Obviously, it was a tragedy, I wouldn't negate that or his feelings for her, but it couldn't have been her that had lain the hex at Whittle Inn's door.

That meant one less suspect.

It was getting late. Or it was late. It might even have been early. The clock on my dashboard was behaving strangely, the numbers rolling and flashing as though they couldn't make up their mind what time it was. But never mind that, I didn't even know what *day* it was anymore. I just needed to get everyone back to the inn—where no doubt it was still three fifty-eight—and put an end to this whole thing once and for all.

I switched off the ignition. There was a dull clunk from the engine.

I frowned. That had *not* sounded healthy.

Deciding to ignore it, I opened my door, welcoming the sudden rush of fresh air and understanding exactly what Venus had meant by the atmosphere being cloying in the van. It was a confined space, and the five of us plus Sampson were breathing the same air.

I hopped out and stretched, watching as Venus tippy-tapped the twenty yards or so up the hill to the toll house. There was a *For Sale* placard outside and the windows had been securely boarded up. That surprised me. Quirky little houses like this one, with all the local history attached, tended to sell quite well despite—by dint of obvious necessity where toll houses were concerned—being set right on the road.

I followed her up the hill, curious to see the building for myself. There was a large wooden noticeboard attached above the main door, hand painted, to notify travellers of the cost to use the road. I read the inscription.

"By an act of the seventh year of King George the Third," I read, "the following tolls are to be paid at this gate for every time of passing. For every carriage whatsoever with four wheels, fourpence. With less than four wheels, tuppence—"

"Cheaper if you've lost a wheel along the way, then," Venus sniffed.

"—for every horse, mare, gelding, mule or ass, laden or not laden, drawing or not drawing, one penny—"

"That would have soon mounted up."

"—for every ox, bull, cow, steer or heifer, a ha'penny. For every calf, swine, sheep or lamb, a farthing," I finished. "Blimey. You'd have been bankrupt if you passed along this road with a flock of sheep."

Venus stood in front of the house and pulled her yak jacket tighter, her long sleek pigtails blowing freely in the wind. She still looked immaculate even in this weather, while my red mane had gone into frizz mode and was tangled in my eyelashes. I pulled a couple of strands of hair out of my mouth and smoothed it back, longing for a scrunchie. Right now, I probably bore more than a passing resemblance to Delilah than I'd ever have thought possible.

"What do you know about this girlfriend?" I asked, as Delilah and Marissa traipsed towards us. I was pleased to see Gertie had remained in the van.

Marissa looked worried. "Is everything alright?" She pointed at the deserted building. "She's definitely—?"

"Dead." I nodded. "According to Venus."

"How?" Marissa asked what we were all keen to know.

Venus sighed in exasperation. "I don't know all the details."

"Did it happen while they were together?" I asked, "or after they'd split up?"

"While they were together," Venus said.

"It broke his heart," Delilah said, and we all looked at her.

"I thought you said you didn't know anything about it?" I said.

She stared in wonder at the house. "I don't. But now that I think back to it, the way he acted whenever we passed this way ... and sometimes we used to go out of our way to travel along this road even though there's a much better one that runs parallel to this ..."

"You think he was paying his respects?" Marissa asked, and Delilah nodded.

"Poor Silvan," I said. I hated to think of him feeling sad.

"It was a long time ago," Venus sniped. "I'm sure he's over it by now."

Delilah squared her shoulders. "You really should let go of some of that bitterness, my love."

I looked from one to the other, surprised that soft Delilah had spoken out, but she was right. Venus evidently had a bit of a chip on her shoulder.

Venus wrinkled her nose in my direction as though I were a bad smell she was taking issue with. "He certainly got over me fast enough."

"Now wait a minute," I protested. "I'm fairly sure there was a lengthy gap between you and me." I pointed at Marissa. "I mean, when I met him—"

"We were never an item," Marissa interrupted. "I keep telling you that."

I rolled my eyes. "I think the lady doth protest too much."

"Not like that," she said. "Not like you and he are."

"Oh, lovely Alfhild and Silvan," mocked Venus. "A match made in heaven."

"We are!" I snapped. "Or at least I thought we were."

Marissa nodded. "You were!"

"Were?" My face crumpled.

"Are!" Marissa hurriedly added, patting my arm. "You still are!"

"I love him," I lamented quietly. "I thought he loved me."

"Let that be enough," Delilah suggested. "I don't think he loved me. Sad but true."

Venus spoke with quiet fury. "I thought he loved me, but quite clearly he didn't!"

"What happened with you guys?" I sniffed away the tears that threatened to spill over.

Venus waved her hands dramatically. "We met. We danced. We had long, passionate nights. Full of excitement and fire and magickal sparks!"

"Oh, I say," said Delilah. "That does sound like fun."

"Didn't you?" Venus checked.

"Good gracious, no. Nothing like that. We had long walks and longer talks. He spent a lot of time away. It was nice though."

"And you?" Venus narrowed her eyes at Marissa, who shot a wary glance my way.

"We didn't—" she started to say.

Venus dismissed her. "And you?" She pointed at me.

"Well—" I stammered, unsure how to proceed. There was always fire and magickal sparks with Silvan and me, mostly because when we were together, we were invariably taking aim at villains.

"Pffft," Venus didn't wait for my response. "I can tell you now," she said, her accent becoming thicker by the minute, "it will be *my* kiss that wakes him up."

"We'll see about that," said Delilah, but Marissa and I could only look at our feet in discomfort. We'd both tried.

We'd both failed.

"If you were his true love," Delilah asked Venus, "how come it didn't last?"

"We were explosive!" Venus replied. "Our love simmered and bubbled like Mount Etna! And then one day? Bloo-bloo-bloo-bloop! It overflowed."

"He dumped you?" I asked. If I sounded slightly catty, it was only because I was beginning to get fed up with hearing about how wonderful everything had been.

My words took the wind out of Venus's sails. "Yes, he did," she admitted.

"But you still hold a candle for him?" Marissa suggested.

Venus drew in a shuddering sigh. "No."

Quite clearly that was a lie. Why else would she have agreed to come all the way down here? She didn't strike me as the sort of woman who did anything out of the goodness of her heart.

But I had no intention of challenging her about it. My days with Silvan were surely numbered too. I could be on the brink of a broken heart myself. It would be unkind to rub another woman's nose in the dirt.

I reached out and stroked her arm. The sooner we returned to the inn, the sooner we would have answers to all of our unspoken questions.

That's when I noticed a light, a glistening ball of energy, floating at about chest height, just in front of the door to the toll house. I waved my hand, directing the other women's attention towards it.

"What is that?" Delilah asked, and Venus leaned forwards, squinting at it. Only Marissa's eyes widened. She recognised a ghost light when she saw one.

I motioned everyone to be quiet and moved slowly towards it. "Come forth," I said. "You are safe with us."

The light bobbed up and down, elongated and popped like a bubble. A young woman, pale and translucent, appeared before us. She had shoulder-length, dark blonde hair with a distinctive wave, light eyes that had either been blue or grey, I would say, and a pleasant although not traditionally beautiful face. Her nose was a little on the crooked side, and her chin a little rounded. More pretty than supermodel. At a guess, she'd been in her early twenties when she'd passed away.

"Greetings," I said softly. "I'm Alfhild Daemonne."

"I heard you all talking about Silvan." She floated a little closer. "I couldn't quite believe my ears."

"You're Silvan's lost love?" I wanted to make certain I hadn't called forth any old spirit who'd been hanging around.

She moved between us, scrutinising our faces. "How long has it been? Time has no meaning here. I'm just waiting... waiting... bored out of my mind."

Delilah reached out as though she would touch the younger woman. "What are you waiting for?" she asked, her voice husky with awe.

The young woman came to a stop. "I don't know." She sounded surprised, as though it had never occurred to her.

"What happened to you?" I asked.

She turned to stare at the tollhouse. "Dodgy electrics. The wiring in that place was lethal. Probably the last time anyone had looked at it properly had been the nineteen sixties." She sighed, an unhappy wistful sound. "I had an attack of the munchies late one evening and managed to electrocute myself when I tried to plug in the toaster."

"Oooh!" All of us grimaced in unison.

"Sorry to hear that," I said.

"Yeah. It kind of cut short my plans, you know? I had so many plans."

"What's your name?" Delilah asked.

"Margaret," the young woman said. "Margaret Patricia Downey. A nice old-fashioned name. My friends called me Maggie. Silvan called me Mags."

"You don't fancy a road trip do you, Maggie?" I asked.

"A road trip?" Maggie beamed at me. "Ooh, yes! I love new adventures and it's been so long since I had one."

"Congratulations, Alfhild," Venus said. "You have a full house of Silvan's ex-lovers."

CHAPTER FIFTEEN

I listened to the babble of excited woman-chatter as I loaded everyone back into the van. Gertie was whinging about something, but I didn't tune into it; my mind was on the clunk I'd heard right before I'd parked up and turned the ignition off. You see, I'd heard a terribly similar sound earlier today—or whatever day it had been—right before I'd had to call the Devon Automobile Recovery Service out to rescue me.

"So, Alf is the latest girlfriend," Delilah was saying, "and before that, it was Marissa who was the-girlfriend-that-wasn't—"

"I wasn't!" Marissa protested.

"It all sounds jolly complicated." Maggie was struggling to get a word in edgeways.

"In my day they'd have called him a gigolo."

"Grandmama?" I peered past Delilah, whom I

was helping into the back of the van. The voice did indeed belong to Gwyn. Perhaps she'd decided to show herself in solidarity with the new spirit I'd invited along.

Great.

I made the introductions. "Grandmama, this is Venus and Maggie. Everyone, this is my great-grandmother, Alfhild Gwynfyre Daemonne, or *Mrs* Daemonne," I said, before she could butt in.

"Pleased to meet you." Maggie did indeed look relieved. I suppose it must be slightly overwhelming to be the only ghosts among humans, even when they're all, without exception, witches.

"I thought now would be a good time to pop in and see everyone, given that you're all finally gathered together. It saves having to have the same discussion over and over again." Gwyn arched an eyebrow at me.

"He's not a gigolo, Grandmama." I frowned at her.

"He's certainly a ladies' man." Before I could protest again, she indicated the others. "But he does have good taste. You are *all* beautiful."

Hmmm.

While the others preened, warming to Gwyn's charm, I slammed the door on them and wandered round to the driver's side. I hopped in and twisted the keys in the ignition.

Click.

My stomach sank like a rock. Just what I was afraid of. *Not now! Not now!*

Taking a breath, I tried again.

Click.

"Come on," I muttered.

Click.

Click.

Click.

"No!" I slapped the steering wheel so hard I hurt my fingers.

Venus, sitting alongside me, looked at me askance. "Problem?" she asked, with the air of a woman who just knew I'd let her down again.

"The engine's been playing up," I explained. "I should have taken it to the garage."

"So why didn't you?" she asked, her temper getting the better of her. "This is so foolhardy! We're here in the dark countryside with nothing around for miles—"

"Oh well, pardon me!" I sniped back. "I had a *little* emergency that I've been trying to sort out. You know? Time freezing on me and the whole of my village falling asleep, including all of the mechanics who work in the garage who might have been able to help me had they all been awake!" I didn't know for sure that they were all asleep, but it sounded feasible. "And this rotten hex, not of *my* doing, has really scuppered things! I've had about three hours sleep in the past ... who knows! It feels like nine thousand years—"

"That's my great-granddaughter, prone to exaggeration," Gwyn chipped in cheerfully from behind.

"—and I've been to London and Bristol and Taunton and Glastonbury, and here I am in Lyme bloomin' Regis, driving a posse of complete—"

"Alf," Marissa interjected gently.

I reined in my snarkiness and blew out a juddering breath. "Yes?" I asked, more reasonably.

"Couldn't you make the van go with some magick?"

"Yes! Fix it with magick!" Delilah chipped in.

Bless them.

"I don't know any I could use," I told them. "Do any of you?"

There was some murmuring from the back, but nobody volunteered anything.

"I didn't complete my degree course," Maggie said. I could hear the note of regret in her voice. "If I had done, I would have taken a couple of modules in auto electro magick."

"Auto electro magick?" Delilah repeated. "I don't think that was a thing in my day."

"Only boys are interested in such things," Venus proclaimed. "Boring magick. Dull. And dirty."

I couldn't disagree with her there, although I'd often thought I should have trained as a magickal plumber—or even a mundane one—there was never a shortage of demand for them. "We should be ashamed," I said. "Six grown witches and not one of us knows how to get a van started."

"Whatever," said Venus. "I don't know how to cut hair either. When I need an expert, I ring one."

She had a point, I suppose. Sighing, I reached into the pocket of my robes and pulled out my mobile phone. I zipped back through the call log until I found the number for the Devon Automobile Recovery Service. I dialled quickly, wondering what time it was in the real world and how long it would take for someone to rescue us.

Fortunately, I was able to pinpoint our whereabouts precisely, thanks to our proximity to the tollhouse, plus Maggie knew the address and postcode, of course. Reassured that the operator was sending a mechanic straight away, I hung up and settled back in my seat, watching the rain slide down the windscreen. It seemed to be getting heavier. I was glad we were inside.

"How long?" Venus asked.

"Not long," I said, although I had no idea what 'not long' equated to.

"I don't feel well," said Gertie.

I closed my eyes, wondering if I could zone the others out and grab forty winks.

"Would you like some water?" Delilah asked.

"No," Gertie said. "I want to be sick."

I uttered a little prayer. *Please make it go away*.

"Alf—" Marissa called.

I opened one eye. Water streamed down the glass in front of my face.

"I think Gertie is feeling a little nauseous."

"She's a ghastly shade of green," Delilah added.

Gertie made a strange bubbling noise. That was all the impetus I needed. I flung open my door and raced around to the back of the van to haul her out. Marissa and Delilah manoeuvred her into my arms and I pulled her towards some nearby bushes.

We were just in time.

I stood there in the dark, in the pouring rain, my hair plastered around my face, my shoulders hunched up around my neck, getting wetter and wetter, waiting for the mechanic to arrive and rubbing poor Gertie's back.

"It will be that hot chocolate that did it," Delilah said, peeking out of the rear door.

"Indeed," said Gwyn. "Alf was a fool to let her have it."

Forty minutes later, glowing lights in my mirrors alerted me to the Devon Automobile Recovery Service. Their van pulled in behind me, and once again I extricated myself from the driver's seat. My clothes were sodden, I smelt like Sampson, and every muscle was beginning to ache. Knowing my luck, I'd probably given myself rheumatic fever and a chill to boot.

I walked towards the mechanic as he jumped out of his van, strapping a torch to his forehead, and stopped in surprise. It was the same chap I'd met before. Peter.

"Hi," I said.

"Hey," he replied.

"Remember me?" I queried.

He squinted towards me, shielding his face against the rain. When he realised who I was, he took an involuntary step backwards. I held my hands up in surrender. "No hexes," I promised. "I just need to get home."

Marissa pushed open the back door. "Sorry Alf, Gertie really needs to get out again."

I indicated the mechanic. "Would you mind?" I asked. "I'm busy."

The mechanic stared in surprise as first Marissa and then Gertie climbed out of the van, rapidly followed by Sampson, who headed straight for the bushes with them.

"Make sure he doesn't run off," I called.

The mechanic took another step back. I laughed. "No, not you. Er ... the dog."

"How many people do you have in that van?" he asked.

Delilah poked her head out, her crown of fern and ivy looking a little dishevelled now. "Hello!"

"Erm, just Delilah and erm ... another lady in the front."

Venus climbed out of the passenger seat. "How long will we be?" she asked. "Only that coffee has gone right through me."

I indicated the bushes.

Gwyn followed her out, floating several inches

above the ground, her form shimmering in the light of the Devon Automobile Recovery Service van.

"Grandmama!" I scolded.

"I need to stretch my legs, my dear."

I tutted. As if she *actually* needed to stretch her legs.

The mechanic's eyes almost popped out of his head. I was impressed that he could actually see Gwyn. Not all mortals are open to ghosts. He scuttled backwards, almost back at his van, and I began to fear he would jump in it and burn rubber to get away from me.

"Please don't leave," I begged. "I'm desperate to get home and I have no idea what is wrong with the engine."

Perhaps I sounded as pathetic as I felt because, casting one wary eye at the motley crew in the bushes, he skirted the van on the opposite side to them and moved to the front.

"Pop the bonnet for me, love," he instructed, "and I'll take a look."

I fumbled in the footwell for the catch, pulled it and watched as he heaved the bonnet up and secured it.

"Turn the ignition on for me," he called. We

repeated the process several times until he told me to stop.

"It seems to be the same issue you were having before. I thought you were going to have it fixed?"

"I've been a bit busy," I said.

He nodded towards the others in the bushes. "So you're all witches, are you?" He laughed nervously as I came to stand by him.

"Yep," I replied. I didn't want to scare him with talk of spells and Snowmageddon and such like again, so I decided to keep quiet.

"A bit late for Halloween, isn't it?"

"A witch is for keeps, not just for Halloween," I quipped.

And that was when Maggie sprang out from the engine, as only a ghost can.

"I think I see what the problem is!" she announced, as the mechanic fainted dead away.

"He'll have a headache in the morning." Maggie sounded most apologetic.

We were all huddled together next to the van waving the mechanic away. Once we'd brought him round and fed him some sugar in the form of the sweeties that Gertie hadn't consumed, he'd worked quickly and proficiently to get the van started. To be fair, his face had been pale, and he'd kept a wary eye on everyone—especially Maggie—but he worked efficiently and, as if by magick, the van had started again in no time at all.

"Get it to the garage," he told me as, once again, I signed his forms promising to pay him silly amounts of money. "And please, the next time you need a mechanic? My name's Peter—"

"Peter," I nodded, keen to make reparations.

"Ask for anyone but Peter," he told me, and took his leave.

As his taillights faded into the darkness, I turned to Maggie. "You really need to rethink the way you interact with the public at large. You scared the living daylights out of him."

Gwyn snorted. "Ignore her, Margaret. Alf's own interaction isn't all it could be at times."

Maggie smiled, a little ruefully. "Sorry. I haven't had a lot of experience with mortals of late."

"He ate all my sweets," grumbled Gertie.

"I don't think he ate them *all*, darling," Marissa said. "You didn't have that many left."

"I had loads left and now they're all gone! I want my sweets!"

Delilah shuffled into the back of the van. "Let me have a look. I'm sure he didn't have many."

"Leave my sweets alone!" shrieked Gertie. I found myself thanking our misfortune of being parked up in such a rural area. Gertie's crying could wake the dead, let alone a bunch of unsuspecting ordinary humans. "They're all gone!"

"Well either I can leave them alone or they're all gone. Only one of those statements can be true," Delilah chirruped.

"They're gone!"

"Kid!" barked Venus, flashing her wand, "If you don't shut up, I'm a-making you gone too."

Someone needed to take charge. Wearily, I realised it would have to be me. "Whoa, Venus!" I stepped between them as Gertie began to wail, and held my hands up to placate everyone. "I appreciate we're all tired, but let's just simmer down—"

"It's that annoying kid who needs to simmer. In a pot over a large open fire," Venus harrumphed and stuffed her wand back into her robes. "Keep her quiet," she said to Marissa. "I've had enough for one day."

Marissa bundled Gertie into the van and Gertie began to cry again. "My doggie! My doggie!"

"Kid," Venus warned.

Gertie piped down.

Sampson.

I walked back towards the bushes, whistling. "Sampson?" I called. "Yoo-hoo! Here boy! Sampson? Who's a good boy?"

He bounded out of the foliage at top speed and I caught him by the collar and lifted him into the van. He felt slimy to the touch.

Once I had everyone inside, I secured the back doors, jumped into my seat and started the engine. To my relief, the van roared into life straight away.

"How far now?" Delilah asked. I could only be grateful for her patience thus far; she'd been part of my entourage for hours.

"It's about sixteen miles or so," I said, and began a three-point turn to get us back on the main drag.

"What is that stink?" Venus asked.

I sniffed.

"Urgh," Marissa groaned from the back.

"Phew," said Gertie.

"It's the dog," Venus said.

Delilah called Sampson over, bent her head and took a closer sniff. "Oh gracious, yes! He must have rolled in something."

"May the goddess have mercy," I begged, wiping my sticky hand over my robes.

Chris Rea was singing about driving home for Christmas and how he couldn't wait to see someone's face. At that moment, I could happily have strangled him and everyone within a twenty-mile radius.

Bah humbug!

CHAPTER SIXTEEN

I drove slowly through the grey twilight land of a sleeping Whittlecombe, raking my gaze left and right, looking out for any signs of life. I spotted several dogs scavenging in bins, but apart from that, nothing living moved. As I'd suspected, the heavy rain we'd encountered on the outskirts of Lyme Regis had turned into sleet as we'd crossed the boundary between Dorset and Devon, and the sky had lightened to this peculiar heavy colour that hurt my eyes.

My companions began to stir as it became obvious we were arriving at our final destination. The van's tyres crunched along the gravel drive and I manoeuvred it into its habitual space at the side of the inn. When I pulled on the handbrake and turned the ignition off, I rode a wave of seasickness, as though my body thought we were still moving.

Despite the silence, my ears rang with the remembered noise of the engine.

"We're home," I announced and unclipped my seatbelt.

Gertie groaned. "I don't feel well."

I hurried around to the back of the van and helped everyone out, grabbing hold of Sampson's lead before he could scurry off. "First things first. You're having a bath, young man."

"I'll do it," said Marissa. "I want to put Gertie in the shower and probably get in myself as well. I reek."

I couldn't disagree. I think we all did, but it was worse for Marissa and Gertie as they'd been huddled up with Sampson for the past fifty minutes. Delilah had refused to have him anywhere near her, evidently a fair-weather animal lover, after all.

I handed Sampson over and took charge of the throws and cushions that had been piled in the back. Everything would need washing now, and while I had no intention of doing that at this moment, I didn't intend to leave it in the van so that it could corrupt the air in there even further.

"Come this way." I led everyone around the front of the inn to the main entrance, Gwyn bringing up the rear. Marissa and Gertie disappeared up the stairs, Gertie whinging about her 'tummy' with every step she took. I led the others past Archibald, still asleep on the reception desk, and through the bar and dining area towards the back passage. I could see nothing had changed anywhere.

"This is the kitchen, the absolute heart of Whittle Inn," I said. "There's winter vegetable broth simmering on the stove there, if anyone would like some." I hefted the pile of cushions in my arms. "I'll just take care of these and I'll be right back."

"Alfhild—" Gwyn called after me.

"Just give me two minutes, Grandmama," I shot back. "I need to get rid of these smelly things."

I dumped my pile of laundry in the utility room, stripped off my cloak and flung it on top, and returned to the kitchen in double-quick time. The others were still standing awkwardly in the middle of the room, waiting for me.

"You don't fancy the broth?" I asked.

"We were just having a conflab," Gwyn said.

Delilah nodded. "Maggie really wants to see Silvan, and we were wondering whether ... well ... should we ... do you think ..."

"Shall we just get the kissing thing over and done with?" Venus drove straight to the point.

"Oh." My head was so fuddled with exhaustion

I'd almost forgotten why I'd gathered these women around me. I had assumed the mantle of innkeeper, intent on making everyone comfortable after a long journey. I was slightly taken aback that they wanted to get on with things, but why stand on ceremony?

"Yes, let's do that." I walked to the kitchen door. "We'll take the back stairs."

We climbed up, coming face to face with the massive Irish wolfhound on the landing. He dipped his head and moved aside as I approached. I gazed at him in wonder. He really did think he'd been guarding Silvan and Charity.

"Good boy," I told him and pushed open the bedroom door. The others gathered around me and peered inside. The curtains were half closed, but I'd left the bedside light burning. The soft glow spilled around the room, catching the shine on Mr Hoo's feathers.

"Oh," exclaimed Maggie, staring only at Silvan. "He's older. But still so handsome!"

"Like the devil," Venus glowered.

"I always knew he'd grow into his looks," Delilah smiled.

"So, what do we do?" Venus asked.

I stepped into the room and the others followed me. We gathered around the bed as though he were about to draw his last breath, although clearly he wasn't. His skin glowed with rugged health and he looked tanned and windswept, as he always did after spending time away on one of his secret missions. There was still dust in his hair, from the Sahara or somewhere, perhaps. I reached down and smoothed a stray lock away from his face.

Please let this work, I begged. *Bring him back to me. To us.*

"You just need to kiss him," I said. "The hex said a true love's kiss. I don't know any other way to interpret that."

I moved out of the way, retreating to the wall next to the bedroom door and standing with my back against it to allow the others to step closer. Delilah was first. She bent her head, hesitated, and straightened up again. "It doesn't feel right," she said, "kissing him while he's asleep."

"I'm inclined to agree with you," Gwyn said. "It's all incredibly distasteful."

"Grandmama." I shot her a warning look.

Venus had no such qualms. "It's just a kiss," she said and brushed Delilah aside. "Not even full on. Just give him a peck. I'm certain he wouldn't mind if he was awake."

"That's true," Maggie said, and I had to agree with them.

Venus took Delilah's place and demonstrated, leaning over and kissing him full on the lips. She left her mouth there for a couple of seconds, then righted herself and stared down at Silvan's face.

"Hmpf," she grunted. "Nothing."

I couldn't tell whether the 'nothing' referred to the fact that Silvan hadn't moved, or that the earth had not moved for Venus either.

She stepped away, frowning, and I realised that she had fully believed that her kiss would be the one to wake Silvan from his slumber. I quelled the selfish little thrill inside me that sang, *ner ner ner ner ner*. Silvan's true love evidently wasn't Venus, and for that, I was grateful.

Delilah glanced first at Venus, then at me, and finally dipped her head. Her kiss was short and perfunctory. Silvan didn't so much as twitch.

"Well." She exhaled as she moved away. "I wasn't expecting it to be me."

All eyes were on Maggie now, but there was one obvious problem.

Ghosts can't kiss the living. Not in the ordinary sense.

"What do I do?" she asked me, flitting around the bed in sudden agitation.

"I don't think there's anything you can do," I told her, "except go through the motions."

She hovered next to him and reached out her hand to stroke his hair, much as I had done. "His hair is so much longer than it was," she said. "And these lines around his eyes—"

I loved those little lines. They crinkled when he was amused.

"—they weren't there before. And his physique," Maggie continued, "he's still wiry, but more muscular. And his hands"—she gazed down in wonder and curled her fingers through his, although he would never have been able to feel it—"I can only imagine what they have done and where they have been."

She knelt beside the bed and looked down at him for a long time.

We waited, each of us respecting this moment for her, giving her the space to remember the good times and Maggie and Silvan's love for each other. Finally, she leaned forward and kissed him.

Nothing happened. Both Silvan and Mr Hoo carried on sleeping. There were no sounds from next door. Charity slept on. The clock on my bedside table remained stuck at three fifty-eight.

I slumped against the wall and studied my feet, at a complete loss.

It was Venus who articulated all our thoughts. "If it's not one of us, then who is it?"

CHAPTER SEVENTEEN

Venus, Delilah, Maggie, Gwyn and I retreated to the kitchen, surrounded by dozens of dogs. All of the visiting dogs, in fact, with the exception of the Irish wolfhound who had remained upstairs, and Sampson who was still in the bath.

I dispensed some treats for the hungry hounds, and this time I didn't have any problem persuading the mortals to partake of a bowl of broth. In fact, we managed to eat two bowls each as well as polish off a dozen rounds of Florence's fresh crusty bread between us, spread thickly with salted butter.

"I needed that," I said, standing up to collect the bowls so that I could wash up.

"Me too," said Delilah. "I thought I was about to fade away. Do you think your chef would let me have the recipe?"

"I'm absolutely sure I could persuade him," Gwyn told her.

"If we ever manage to wake them up," Venus chipped in.

"Anyone for tea?" I asked, channelling my inner Florence. "I expect there's some cake somewhere too." The chocolate Yule log wouldn't last much longer.

"You English. Do you have anything stronger than tea?" Venus asked.

I hesitated. "I do. I'm just a little worried that we might have to drive somewhere else and pick someone else up …"

"*You* might have to," Venus sniffed. "But *I'm* not going anywhere. And even if I do, I won't be driving."

Delilah smirked. "Good idea, Venus. You could stay here and look after the little one and all the dogs, I suppose."

Venus's eyes widened in horror. "On second thoughts, I'll have some coffee."

Delilah and I laughed. After a moment, Venus joined in. It was the first time I'd seen her look anything other than furious or bored. Our shared amusement provided a wonderful release from the built-up tension. We were all tired, but at least we had a little more fuel in the tank.

Only Maggie was quiet, slumping against the worktops, moving utensils around with the telekinetic energy that spirits can utilise.

"Are you alright?" I queried. It's a strange question to ask a ghost, but they have thoughts and feelings like the rest of us. I imagined that she was feeling sad because she'd been so cruelly reminded of what had been taken away from her. If she hadn't died when she did, who knew what might have happened. She and Silvan could have travelled the world together, married, had children. Anything was feasible.

If Maggie hadn't died, neither Venus nor Delilah, nor myself come to that, would have met him and had any kind of relationship with him. He might not have been engaged in his current line of work had Maggie survived. Perhaps he would have stayed on the straight and narrow.

I kind of doubted that last bit somehow. Silvan had been born to be a dark witch.

"I lied," Maggie said, her voice small and quiet in the kitchen. She could hardly be heard above the noise of the oven, the roar of the kettle and the bubbling of the pans on the stove.

"I'm sorry?" I said.

"I lied," she repeated, a little louder, catching the attention of Venus and Delilah, still lounging at the kitchen table.

"About what?" I asked.

"Are you not Silvan's lost love?" Venus demanded to know. "Aye-aye-aye. I knew there was something!"

If she *had* known anything was amiss, she hadn't shared it with the rest of us.

"No, I am," Maggie reassured us, her eyes wide and earnest. "Kind of."

"Kind of?" I repeated.

"Spill the beans," Delilah said. "Truth will out."

Maggie sighed. "I am the 'lost love' that you refer to. But … the fact is that … Silvan and I … we had already broken up *before* I died."

"Oh." I didn't know what else to say.

"Ha!" Venus said. "I knew it." I glared at her. Venus knew nothing, except after the event.

"Was it you or him—?" I felt compelled to ask.

Maggie knew what I meant. "Me. We broke up on my instigation. I broke Silvan's heart."

"Why would you do that?" Gwyn sounded most put out. I think love affairs had been a vastly different proposition in her day.

Maggie shrugged as though it were of no matter, but I could see the pain in her eyes. "I'd met someone else. An electrician."

We all studied Maggie in mute fascination.

"An electrician? That's kind of ironic," I said. Given the way she had died.

She nodded, her eyes downcast. I feared she might burst into tears, and you know I'm a sucker for a sobbing ghost, but suddenly she tipped her head back and guffawed. "Yes," she struggled to say between peals of laughter. "Yes! You could say that."

Marissa joined us at that moment, leaving Gertie upstairs in Charity's bed with a freshly bathed Sampson and a variety of other canine companions who, bored with our ongoing discussion and lack of activity, had gone in search of the littlest witch.

We sat together, the six of us. I served up tea and coffee and cake and, as we talked and laughed about the mishaps and escapades we had shared with Silvan, one thing became abundantly clear. Wherever he went, Silvan spread a huge amount of joy and love. With his support, each of us had improved our lives, started to maximise our potential, and worked at becoming a better version of ourselves.

But if none of us was Silvan's true love, where-oh-where did that leave us now?

Feeling podged and sleepy, we remained sitting around the table for nearly an hour, content in each other's company. We'd been running through a variety of options, discussing which would be the best avenue to pursue next. One possibility was to turn to Wizard Shadowmender and Wizard Magigi again, and asking for more help. We'd also drawn up a list of every woman we could think of who had ever had anything to do with Silvan in one capacity or another.

From my perspective, that included some particularly dubious names. Meztli, anyone? What about Nadia Cozma? I couldn't see these women mattering to Silvan in any romantic way, but at this stage we weren't prepared to rule anyone out.

"This 'Carina' Delilah mentioned might be worth a look." I tapped the notes in front of me. Someone he had once worked with.

"Where does she live?" Delilah asked.

"Northampton," Venus said.

I mused on this. "That's a pain to get to from here. I don't know if I trust the van to do it."

"I don't want to go in the van no more."

I jumped. Gertie had snuck in while we'd been talking, leading a trail of hounds in her wake.

"What are you doing down here?" Marissa asked. "I thought you were asleep."

"My tummy hurts." Gertie began to cry. "I don't want to go in the van again."

"It's alright," I soothed. "You don't have to. You can stay here with Marissa till you're well again and then we'll get you home." I didn't fancy a road trip that would have to encompass Northampton and London, but I suppose I didn't have a huge amount of choice. It would be much easier if I could leave everyone else at home and travel alone.

"My tummy h-h-hurts!" Gertie sobbed.

"I suppose it is just all the sweet stuff she ate, isn't it?" I asked Marissa. "Not something more serious, like botulism or a burst appendix or something?"

"So unlike you to look on the bright side of life," said Gwyn. "The child clearly has a stomach ache."

"I suppose we could take Gertie to a doctor," I said. "There'll be an emergency clinic open somewhere."

"I don't want to go in the van no more," Gertie repeated. "It smells."

"Well, whose fault is that?" Venus asked.

"If only Millicent were here," I said.

"Who's Millicent?" Delilah wanted to know.

"She's my friend," I explained. "She's a potioner. A brilliant one. I'm sure she'd have been able to fix little Gertie here."

"A clip round the ear would work wonders," Gwyn muttered. "In my day—"

Gertie had been listening to the exchange. "Where is Millicent?" she asked. "Can't she come over?"

"She's asleep," I told her.

Gertie frowned. "Is she asleep because it's night-time?"

"No. She's asleep because everybody is."

"But she could make me better?"

"I'm certain she could."

"Can you wake her up?" She looked up at me, her head tipped back, her huge eyes brimming with tears.

"It may have escaped your notice, kid, but we have been trying to wake everyone up for hours," Venus snapped.

Gertie's frown creased. "Is it because of the true love's kiss?" she asked, her voice laced with fear.

"Yes," Marissa said, kneeling next to Gertie. "I'm sorry that you're caught up in all this. We're doing our best. We have to find out who Silvan's true love is."

"No you don't," Gertie said, her voice virtually inaudible, tipping her face down so we couldn't see it.

"We do, darling. We have to get rid of the bad magick," Marissa explained, rubbing her niece's back.

"I didn't mean it to be bad magick!" Gertie wailed.

I froze. Had I heard that right?

"What did you say?" Marissa asked.

"I said I'm sorry," Gertie repeated. "I didn't think it was bad magick."

I still couldn't speak.

"What do you mean?" asked Delilah. She turned to Marissa, her face a mask of shock. "What does she mean?"

"Gertie?" Marissa coaxed her niece gently. "Do you need to tell us something?"

Gertie seemed tiny in my large kitchen, her chin sinking to her chest. "I did it," she said. "I cast the spell."

We gathered together around the kitchen table once more, but this time all eyes were on Gertie. I gave her a glass of gently warmed lemonade. Somewhere in the recesses of my mind, I remembered my own mother giving me something like that when I was a child to fix an upset tummy. Perhaps more placebo than effective medicine but, with Millicent indisposed, it had to be worth a try.

"Tell us everything," Marissa said, and for once there was an edge of steel to her tone that even Gertie couldn't fail to detect. She sipped a little of her drink.

"I like Silvan," she said. "I liked it when he stayed with us. He played with me."

"He's a nice man," Marissa said.

"I liked it when you used to be friends and he came round to see you," Gertie explained. "I wanted him to stay."

"But he can't stay with me, you know that." Marissa flicked Gertie's hair away from her face. "He's Alf's partner."

"I thought I could make him stay with us. That he could be your love."

I remembered a lesson I'd learned the hard way. "You can't make people love you, Gertie. They either do or they don't. Forced love, magicked love, is not true love."

Gertie sniffed. "I wanted a mummy and a daddy and Christmas presents and a dog." She reached down to stroke Sampson. "And I wished and wished but nothing happened. But then I found a book of magick in the bookshop—"

Marissa clamped her hand to her cheek. "Oh dear."

"And I read about the hex box and I knew I'd seen the hex box before."

"The hex box?" I stood up, casting around for my belongings. "Where's my bag? Wait a second." I rushed into the laundry room and scattered the pile of stinking cushions and throws. Amongst it all I located my bag.

"Here!" I cried, jubilantly waving the box as I re-entered the kitchen. "Is this what you're talking about?"

I set the box on the table in front of Gertie. The others regarded its intricate carvings with fresh interest. Apart from Marissa. "That's mine!" she cried. "I keep it in my underwear drawer. Did you take this from among my things?"

Gertie nodded, her face a picture of misery. "Sorry, Auntie Marissa."

"I didn't know it was a hex box." Marissa picked it up and turned it round and round. "The funny thing is, it was Silvan who gave it to me in the first place. He found it somewhere on his travels, somewhere exotic. He knew I'd like it. A weird curio. I thought it must have been some kind of jewellery box once, but it was completely empty when he gave it to me. Not even this velvet casing." She plucked it out, examining the small square of cloth. It had been roughly cut out from a larger piece of material.

"I put that in there," Gertie said, almost proudly. "The book said to line it with velvet."

"So how did the hex work?" I asked. If we could understand the basics of the spell, surely it would be easier to undo it.

"I had to choose what I wanted to say," Gertie told me, and I could sense her reluctance to tell the whole truth.

I pressed her. "And what you wanted was for Marissa to be with Silvan?"

"Yes. So I chose the sleeping spell because I didn't think that would hurt anyone and I thought Marissa could be the witch heroine and wake him up."

"But you knew he had a girlfriend," Marissa chided her niece. "He told you about Alf."

"I forgot her name," Gertie replied sullenly. She snuck a glance at me. "I wanted you to go to sleep as well. I just wanted Marissa to save him. I didn't know everyone would join in." She looked round at Delilah, Venus, Maggie and Gwyn.

I pulled a face. I had some sympathy with her. She had bitten off far more than she could chew and had thrown herself into some fairly adult spellcasting by accident. There was no way she could have known what she was getting herself into.

"It was a long spell," Gertie continued, cupping her hands and blowing into the space between her thumbs. "You breathe into a gem and you say the words—I had trouble with some of those—and you add your own bit."

"And what was your own bit?" Venus asked, leaning away from Gertie as though she thought the poor child was the devil's spawn. To be honest, there was probably something in that.

"I wanted a doggie."

I loosened a nervy breath. "That's why all the dogs in the village were immune from the spell."

Delilah chuckled. "Powerful magick, that."

"It is indeed." I leaned forward. "You know, Gertie, I do think Silvan will be really impressed with what you have done, although he'd probably tell you to be careful how you meddle. You need to realise that any magick we let loose into the world can have unexpected consequences. Do you know what I mean by unexpected consequences?"

"Things that I didn't mean to happen?" Gertie asked.

I nodded. "That's right. I think you have the makings of a wonderfully powerful and creative witch. But! And this is a big but! You have to learn how to control what you do, and you always have to know what the antidote is, in case things go wrong."

"As they often do," sighed Delilah.

I clasped Gertie's hand. "What I need to know right now is how to undo the spell you cast."

"But you already know!" Gertie frowned, sounding cross that I was choosing to be so stupid.

I shook my head. "What am I missing?"

"True Love's Kiss?" Gertie reminded me. "In the book, it said to put the anti-thingummy in the box with the spell if you wanted to be able to undo it." She smiled at me. "I did that. True Love's Kiss."

I sighed and rubbed my tired eyes. "But we've tried that, Gertie. Every one of us has kissed Silvan and he's still asleep. We don't know who his true love is."

"Not real kissing!" Gertie wrinkled her nose up. "Eww no! Kissing is icky."

"Then what?" I could feel my frustration simmering away like a cauldron about to boil over.

"It's a potion," said Gertie with evident satisfaction. "A True Love's Kiss is a potion."

CHAPTER EIGHTEEN

Three fifty-eight.

"And that's the time that it's always been," I sang, unable to remember what song that was a line from or what the next line should be. That single line repeated on a refrain around my tired, fuzzy head.

We had donned our raincoats and scarves, and brought along Jasper and Sunny—and Sampson at Gertie's insistence. We walked down into Whittlecombe, leaving Gwyn to look after the inhabitants of the inn, of both the canine and non-canine variety. The light, still that intense grey, seemed less gloomy in the village thanks to the illuminated strings of lights that stretched from building to building and across the roads. The large Christmas tree on the green sparkled with its own rainbow-coloured fairy lights, and flashing snowmen and Father Christmases adorned a variety of windows. In front of one house, I could see an oversized inflatable elf jigging around to some music only it could hear.

I led everyone into Millicent's small cottage and, while Jasper and Sunny rushed to Millicent's side and gave her a good face washing and some canine nurturing—to no avail—the rest of us carefully wiped our feet and hung up our coats. "If Millicent doesn't have a copy of the recipe for this potion I wouldn't know where else to look," I whispered.

The others regarded Millicent, lying peacefully on her couch, with curiosity. I plonked Gertie down beside her and set the others to work at once.

Millicent's bookshelves lined the underside of her open-plan staircase, so I asked Venus and Delilah to search through those while Marissa checked out the main bedroom, Maggie took the spare bedroom and I went into the kitchen.

Millicent is one of those super-organised women who labels absolutely everything. Her pantry looked like a library for potion ingredients. There were rows and rows of bottles of all shapes, sizes and colours, and jars and demi-johns on the floor containing all manner of horrors and peculiar items. Every single one of them had a label written in Millicent's neat handwriting describing the contents along with a 'best-before-end-of' date. I knew that once we had the recipe, we would find all the items we needed to create our antidote right here among Millicent's things.

Above her tiny kitchen table was a single shelf with some of her most precious potion recipe books. I had a feeling these had been handed down from her mother and grandmother. The pages were thick and well-thumbed. In places, there were annotations written in a beautiful script, smaller than Millicent's own flourish. The binding of several of these books, with their heavy covers etched in black and gold, had started to unravel and there were numerous loose pages. I took great care to lay each book on the clean table and thumb through gently, searching the table of contents—where there was one—for likely sources, and then the index if nothing else proved fruitful.

I scanned page after page of delightful concoctions. *A Potion to Reduce Wrinkles*. That sounded useful. *A Potion for Dotting the i's and Crossing the t's*. Definitely something I'd be interested in. *A Potion to Aid Sleep*. I paused here and read the details, but it was designed to alleviate the symptoms of insomnia.

A Potion to Illuminate the Darkness. Ooh! Now

that sounded interesting, but I had to draw the line at 'locating a blind goat's eyeballs'.

"I've got something!" Delilah shouted from the living room. I left my book where it was and hurried out. Marissa and Maggie joined Venus and Delilah, kneeling together in front of Millicent's coffee table. Venus ran her finger down the page, reading what she saw there.

I huddled with them, straining to see.

Somnus Hex. This was it!

"Also known as the Sleeping Beauty curse," Venus read aloud. "A spell to be used only in exceptional circumstances due to its tendency to be indiscriminate. Ooh!" She pointed at some bold type. "Look! There's an addendum here from the Ministry of Witches."

"What does it say?" Maggie asked.

"The Ministry of Witches strongly advises against the use of the Somnus Hex in ordinary magickal practice. It is vital that the antidote to the hex—especially when it is elevated to a curse—be included in every circumstance where the spell is cast. In no circumstances should the spell be used by any witch below third degree. We would ultimately encourage interested parties to speak to an advisory member of the Ministry of Witches in the first instance."

"Oops." Marissa gulped and stared in horror at her niece. "What have you done?" she whispered.

Gertie's eyes were huge in her pale face. "I didn't know. I just wanted to try it." Tears welled up. "Now my tummy hurts and I just want to be better. Wake the lady up!" She pointed at Millicent.

"That would be a lot easier if you hadn't conjured up this mess in the first place," Venus said, but given the warmth of her tone, I had a serious suspicion she was beginning to enjoy herself.

"What do we need to do?" Delilah asked. "Does it list the antidote?"

Venus flipped over the page. "True Love's Kiss! It does. Let me see … we need … oh, wow! It's a bit complicated. You need to create a wake-up 'chyme', it says. A magickal alarm clock."

"How do you do that?" I had visions of nurturing my woodwork skills and creating some sort of clunky grandfather clock.

Apparently not.

Venus carried on reading. "To create a chyme, start by steeping thyme in a pint of hot chai—"

"Chai?" Maggie asked.

"It's tea. From India," Delilah nodded. "I love it."

"Would Millicent have chai in her cupboard?" Marissa asked.

"Millicent has everything." I stood up, prepared to start looking.

Delilah stopped me. "You would normally make a good chai from scratch."

"Is there a recipe?" I asked, bending over Venus to take another look.

"No," she said. I shrugged at Delilah.

"I'm pretty sure I can remember how to make it," she smiled. "Black tea mixed with a variety of strong spices."

"Millicent has loads of that kind of thing. When you open her pantry it smells like Asia." I'd never been to India, but I knew what Silvan's clothes smelt like when he returned from such places.

"I'll make the chai, then." Delilah tootled off to the kitchen, happy enough. I heard water run and Millicent's whistly kettle settled onto the stove.

"There'll be thyme in her greenhouse," I said. "Do we need any other herbs?"

"Well ..." Venus scanned the list. "We need seven flakes of sundried raspberry, seven grams of sunflower seeds, seven grams of pink candy floss, seven basil leaves and seven millilitres of concentrated cherry juice. Pour into a blender and mix well."

"I have to say as potions go, this one actually sounds quite nice," I noted in surprise. I'd been on the receiving end of some very strange concoctions from Millicent over the past two years, some of them remarkably unpleasant. I'd given up asking her what she put in them because it could be quite off-putting.

"Ha!" Venus snorted. "I haven't finished yet."

"Go on." I dreaded to hear the rest.

"Seven earthworms—"

"Grim," I said.

"—and the heart of an ox."

I met Marissa's eyes. She pretended to gag. "Ick."

"How are you guys even witches?" Venus roared with laughter. "At least it's not asking you to slay the ox yourself on the night of the new moon or something onerous."

"True," I said, charmed by Venus's amusement. I could see now why Silvan had liked her. She had the constitution of a lion and a devilish sense of humour.

"Oh, I've lost my place." Venus skimmed the page again. "Where was I?"

"The heart of an ox," I prompted.

"Re-blend until a smooth consistency, heat in a cauldron for an hour. Strain the mixture through red silk and decant into a receptacle. Use within three days."

"Right. So, basil and thyme. Maybe if Marissa gets that from the greenhouse, out the back?" I suggested, and Marissa nodded. "I'll go and look through the cupboards in Millicent's kitchen for sundried raspberry, sunflower seeds and concentrated cherry juice. I'm quite sure she'll have those. What else was there?"

Venus rechecked. "Candy floss?"

"Maybe at the shop," I said doubtfully.

"Earthworms."

"Garden," said Marissa.

"The ox heart."

"Maybe in the freezer here, more likely to be in the freezer in the shop." I nodded.

"Well, why don't Maggie and I go to the shop?" Venus suggested. "She can help me look."

"Good idea. Just out of the front door and turn right. Keep going, you can't miss it." I turned for the kitchen. "And don't forget to pay."

"Pay?" Venus looked most put out.

"Rhona and Stan don't make a fortune in that little shop. We don't want to steal their produce."

Venus rolled her eyes. "You're just too much of a goody-two-shoes, Alf."

"They're my friends!"

"Whatever." Venus dismissed the notion of friendship with one wave of her hand. "Anyway, I don't have any cash. I don't carry it. I'm like the Queen."

I groaned. During the past eleventy-hundred hours I'd spent a small fortune. "Take my purse," I told her, digging it out of my pocket.

"What should I do?" Gertie asked.

"Stay away from spell books," Venus suggested and waltzed out of the front door with Maggie floating closely behind.

Gertie stuck out her bottom lip. I could see she wanted to make amends. "Perhaps you could keep an eye on the dogs for me," I suggested. "Stop them bothering poor Millicent while she's asleep." Jasper, bless him, had been trying to get his mistress's attention. He stood with his front paws in her lap, licking her ear. Sunny lay on Millie's feet, rolled tightly into a ball. Sampson had been investigating Millicent's wool stash, and several skeins of it were now unravelled on the floor.

Millicent wouldn't thank me for that.

"I'll do that," Gertie said, and set about trying to catch Jasper's attention while I joined Delilah in the kitchen. She was busy weighing out sticks of cinnamon on Millicent's old-fashioned scales.

"How's it going?" I asked.

"Fine. I quite envy Millicent's supplies. Her spices are of excellent quality. Very fresh."

"I think she imports them specially. She has contacts in India, Sri Lanka, South America and China. Witches she's worked with over the years."

"I'll have to pick her brains." Delilah tipped the cinnamon sticks into the pestle and mortar where the other spices waited. She began to pummel the heavy pestle into the smooth bowl, crushing seeds and corns and sticks viciously. The fragrance was incredible. Sweet, yet dry and musky, hot and peppery, evocative of a dusty continent.

"Whew!" I said, "You could get high off that."

I began to rummage in Millicent's cupboards. I found the raspberry flakes easily enough. How could you miss that colour? And an enormous jar of sunflower seeds. Concentrated cherry juice proved more problematic until I searched the fridge and there, as luck would have it, was a clear bottle with the remnants of a small batch Millicent had made over the summer.

"I hope it's still drinkable," I muttered as I un-stoppered it and sniffed the contents. It smelt sour, but I suppose that's cherries for you.

"I'm not sure it matters, given what else we're adding to the mix," Delilah smiled. The kettle began to whistle and she quickly filled up Millicent's pint jug to create the tea before adding the spice mix, stirring it well with a battered wooden spoon.

"Great timing!" Marissa arrived with a bunch of thyme and a handful of basil leaves. "I couldn't remember how much basil was needed, so I brought a load. And look what else I found out there."

I peered at the large pickling jar Marissa held in her hand and quickly recoiled. "Eww! Is that what I think it is?" It was half full of dark liquid. When she swirled it around, what I had first taken to be strands of fat spaghetti turned out to be the ringed bodies of plump earthworms.

"It is! Millicent has stores of everything for any occasion. There are frogs in brine, eyeballs aplenty and other things I didn't recognise. Body parts, I think."

"She's a strange woman," I acknowledged.

"What about the basil? Is this enough? I'm amazed she's able to grow it out there at this time of year."

"I expect she uses magick," Delilah suggested. "I

know I have to turn to it when the winter days are long and my plants begin to feel sad. I like to cheer them up with a little artificial sunshine."

"I think it was seven leaves of basil we needed," I said. "Let me grab the recipe book so we can make certain on quantities."

I collected the book from the coffee table, smiling at Gertie as I passed, and brought it into the kitchen. We huddled around it again, re-reading the instructions. "A cauldron. Millicent's cauldron is on the floor of the pantry," I mentioned. "We can use that."

"What's this?" Marissa pointed to a short section that Venus hadn't mentioned. "After the heart of an ox?"

"Drop the crystal used in the original Somnus Hex into the mixture," I read, crinkling my brow at this new instruction. "What crystal?" We flipped back a page to study the instructions for the Somnus Hex, and there, taking primary importance among the ingredients, was 'a small rose quartz'.

My heart sank. Gertie had created the potion at Marissa's home in Tumble Town. Presumably she had left the crystal there. Did that mean I would have to go all the way back to London just to try to locate a tiny stone?

I popped my head around the door. "Gertie?" I

called. She glanced up, fear in her eyes. I knew that look. It was one that had regularly manifested itself on my own face as a teenager, at home with my mother. *Am I in trouble again?*

"You're doing a good job there, with the dogs," I smiled. Jasper had his head in her lap now and appeared to be trying to tell her something. Sunny was still settled on Millicent's legs, and Sampson lay on the opposite side to Jasper, sound asleep, as Gertie fondled his ears.

"Think back to when you cast the spell," I said, trying to keep my tone casual. "Do you remember using a crystal?"

"Yes," Gertie nodded. "I used one of Auntie Marissa's stones. She has lots."

"A rose quartz?" I asked.

"A pink one."

"Great." I nodded. "And what did you do with the crystal once you'd cast the spell?"

Gertie regarded me as though I was made of green cheese. "The crystal *is* the spell."

"The crystal is the spell?" For all I knew she was speaking in tongues. I didn't understand. I moved back into the kitchen to take another look at the book, my head aching.

"She's right," said Delilah. "Look. It says here,

you hold the crystal in a loosely clamped fist and say the spell into the hole there." I remembered the way Gertie had clasped her hands together and blown between her thumbs while we'd all been sitting around my kitchen table. "You breathe onto the crystal until all of your intent is embedded there," Delilah continued.

Now I understood. "That's all well and good, but we still need the crystal." I popped my head back around the door. "So, what happened to the crystal, Gertie?"

"You should know." Now it was Gertie's turn to look puzzled. "You said you opened it."

"The box?" I clarified. "Yes, I opened the box."

"It was *in* the box," Gertie's voice started to rise.

I wanted to keep the situation calm, but we had to be talking at cross purposes. "There was nothing in the box. Nothing at all."

"There was! I put the stone in the box." Gertie's face was starting to turn thunderous, her brow low over her eyebrows, her eyes flashing. She was on the verge of another tantrum. Jasper shifted warily but didn't forsake his comfortable seat.

"But—" I stopped, knowing I was upsetting her. Why would she lie now? She had nothing to gain.

I reconsidered those micro-moments after I'd

opened the box. The rush of raspberry- and cherry-scented air as though someone—a child as it turned out—had exhaled on me. And then what? I had zoned out. Mere moments of absence. I hadn't heard the box fall to the table, but I had been convinced that something had dropped to the floor.

And yet, when I'd searched, I hadn't been able to find anything.

I would need to go back and have another look.

It would help to know exactly what I was looking for.

"This stone that you used for the spell, Gertie?" I asked. "How big would you say it was?"

Gertie wiggled her shoulders. "Not very big. I was afraid that Auntie Marissa would notice it had gone missing and that I would get into trouble."

I nodded. That made sense.

"It was thin."

"Like a chip off a stone?" I asked.

"Yes!" She had calmed down, seeming pleased that she could help me with this at least. "It was a really little bit. Thin but long. Like"—she screwed up her eyes trying to imagine a comparison—"not long like a chewing gum stick—"

Why had that come to her mind? "But slim like that?" I guessed.

"Yes."

"But not as long." We were getting somewhere. "Half as long as a stick of chewing gum?" I suggested.

"No."

"Less?"

"Yes."

"Alrighty then, that helps lots. Thank you." I gave her a reassuring wink and turned back to the others. The potion was beginning to smell now, sweet, almost appetising. That would change when the other ingredients went in. "I'm going to nip out to the post office," I told them, "and see if I can locate the crystal Gertie used."

"The magick ingredient," Delilah said.

"It certainly seems like it," I nodded.

CHAPTER NINETEEN

I took a brisk stroll from Millicent's towards the post office and bumped into Venus and Maggie heading back to Hedge Cottage.

Venus waved a hessian bag at me. "Success!"

"An ox heart?" I asked. I'd forgotten to check Millicent's freezer.

"Yes! And a dozen bags of pink candyfloss."

"Well, that was lucky!" I couldn't quite believe Venus had found candyfloss at Whittle Stores.

"We had a rummage in the stockroom," Maggie confided. "I think it's a bit out of date."

"It'll be alright. Perhaps a little granular. Must have been left over from Guy Fawkes night," I said. That would be the perfect time to have candyfloss.

Maggie agreed. "Better than nothing."

"Are you going to see to the ox heart?" I asked Venus.

She scowled at me in response. "See to it?"

"Chop it up and blend it," I clarified.

Venus closed her eyes in exasperation. "My darling, I *don't* cook."

That's why she was so beautifully slender. "The thing is ..." I tried to wheedle my way around her using my plaintive voice, "Delilah and Marissa are both vegetarian. In fact, Delilah is a vegan. It would be really helpful if you would sort it for them."

Venus waggled her long fingernails at me. "I *don't* cook."

"It's not really cooking," I protested.

Venus was having none of it. "I don't *work* in the kitchen at all."

Maggie snorted. "What do you do then? How do you eat?"

"I go out. I have people cook for me."

"This isn't real cooking anyway. It's potions." Maggie attempted to appeal to Venus's dark side. "It's proper witch business."

"Don't worry," I said. "I'll do it. I don't mind."

I didn't like the idea of chopping up a raw heart either, but it had to be done. I knew Silvan wouldn't have batted an eyelid. He'd expect the same from me.

As if she could read my mind, Venus sneered.

"Alright, alright. If it makes this whole sorry mess go any quicker, I'll do it. What are you up to, anyway, Alfhild?"

"I need to find an ingredient you neglected to tell us about." I couldn't help the dig. When Venus only looked blank, I went on. "Apparently, a crystal is used in the original Somnus hex that also has to be utilised in the antidote. Gertie swears blind it was in the box. It must have dropped out when I opened it. I'm going to the post office to look for it."

"Do you need another pair of eyes?" Maggie asked. "I'm happy to help you scout round."

That might come in handy. "That's great, thanks," I said and, nodding at Venus as she moved away, I led Maggie to the entrance of the post office.

"It's a really old-fashioned place," I told her as I pushed the door open, "and I love it for that. It probably hasn't changed in over eighty years."

She looked up as the bell above us tinkled in its light, friendly way. "That's the kind of thing I miss," she said. "The sheer ordinariness of a way of life. Being human, I suppose."

I turned to look at her, noticing her misty eyes. "It must be hard to adapt," I said. "The ghosts at the inn have often told me so. I promise they do get there eventually."

"Do you think they have adapted well because they have found a purpose?" Maggie asked me, following behind as I threaded my way through the shelving units to the back of the shop.

"I think that's certainly the case with many of them. Florence loves the inn, loves being busy, loves baking and housekeeping ... in fact she just loves life generally. She's an absolute joy."

I smiled, hoping it wouldn't be long till I would see her again. "Then I have Zephaniah and Archibald and Ned and a whole host of ghosts who form part of the Wonky Inn Ghostly Clean-up Crew. They all seem happy enough to stick around. I periodically check with them," I grinned, "kind of like a staff appraisal. I like to make sure they still want to remain on this plane, working at the inn with me."

"And if they don't?"

I raised my eyebrows. "I'm pleased to say that rarely happens, but if it does, I can send them to the next."

We'd reached the table where I'd been sitting at three fifty-eight who knew how many days ago. I pulled out the chair so I could sit down. I wanted to be at the level I had been when I opened the box.

"What's there? In the next plane?"

I turned my head slowly to take a better look at her. "I don't know," I told her honestly. "I don't think anyone knows."

She inhaled deeply, not that ghosts breathe, but the sound of it filled the room. She wouldn't be able to smell the mustiness that I loved so much. "New adventures," she said, her voice soft.

"I would love to think so."

She held my gaze a moment and then hurriedly looked away. "Right!" She clapped her hands as though to dispel a frisson of nerviness. "What exactly am I looking for?"

"It's a piece of pink quartz, thin and about an inch long. Maybe less."

I swept the palms of my hands across the table in front of me, disturbing a fine layer of dust and a few scraps of paper but not much else, so I pushed the chair back and dropped into a crouch until my eyes were level with the top of the table. Absolutely nothing to see.

Maggie was searching around on the floor. I pulled the wastepaper bin out from under the table and tipped the contents onto the tabletop, examining every piece of litter and replacing it into the bin. Paper, pieces of plastic wrap, envelopes, the plastic backing from postage stamps, a pen, a banana skin. Yuck.

My heart skipped to see the flash of something shiny. But it was too red and turned out to be a half-sucked boiled sweet.

Double yuck.

By the time I'd replaced everything, Maggie had sunk to her knees and then lain flat against the floor, peering under the shelving units. She was better at that than me. I couldn't have done it without sneezing or coughing. There had to be dust monsters living under there.

What we really needed was a torch. I looked around at the products on sale with no success until I remembered I had my wand on me. The goddess knows why I hadn't thought of using it before, but I suppose when I'd been searching previously, I'd been a bit half-hearted about it. I hadn't realised it was imperative to find whatever it was I imagined had dropped from the box. I lit the wand up and knelt down, sweeping it backwards and forwards. "*Revelare*," I said, and finally something glinted in the corner of my eyes.

"There!" Maggie turned and pointed, and I crawled over to take a better look. Wedged between the floorboards, the slim pink edge not immediately noticeable, was the crystal.

"Hoorah!" I said, trying to slip my thumbnail down the side and prise it out. A splinter of wood stabbed me and I recoiled. "Ouch!"

"Here, this strikes me as a job for Superghost." Maggie winked at me and flicked a finger at the quartz. I watched, sucking on my thumb as, without touching the crystal at all, Maggie was able to wiggle it out of its tight space. It rose and floated through the air towards me. She nodded as I held my hand out. The stone landed gently on my palm, ticking the sensitive skin there, radiating a little magickal energy.

"Thank you."

She held my gaze and I didn't immediately move. Her eyes burned with an intensity that made me want to look away. There was a question there. It made my heart ache to see it.

She would not be put off, however. "You could send me over."

My breath stuck in my throat. "If that's what you really wanted," I said. "If there was nothing else to keep you here—"

"There's nothing."

"Silvan—"

"Was not my love at the time I passed," Maggie said.

"But from what Venus and Delilah have told us, he must still have some feelings for you," I protested.

Maggie frowned. "Holding a candle to a memory of a love long ago is different to still being *in* love. There is nothing for us—Silvan and I—on this plane. There is nothing at all for me here. I have no purpose. No family to watch over. My travelling days are done."

"You could join us at the inn," I offered, although I knew that would never work.

She had made her mind up. "No. I've been hanging around in that old toll house for thirteen years and I'm bored with it. It's not enough for me. I want to go in search of new adventures. I want to find out what waits for me on the other side."

Whenever I had sent someone over in the past, I had tried not to let emotion get the better of me, but now tears began to prickle in my eyes. I had known this woman for a matter of hours, but something about her importance to Silvan made me reluctant to send her away. Not without him seeing her.

She must have understood my doubts. "This is not about Silvan; it is about me," she reminded me. "He and I were already over by the time of my accident. We would never have worked out. I'm certain that had I lived on to be an old lady, he would have forgotten me quickly enough."

"Perhaps."

"Undoubtedly." She thought for a moment. "It might be kindest not to tell him you found me."

"I would never want to lie to him," I frowned.

"You have a kind heart, Alf. The thing to remember, always, is that everything in life happens for a reason. Silvan and I split up. He found something new with Delilah, and then temporarily with Venus. Those relationships have changed him, shaped and moulded him. They are what led him eventually to you." She held out a hand. I wished I could take it. "I know Marissa feels the same way that I do. You and Silvan are meant to be. What you have is entirely natural."

I drew in a juddering breath, a tear spilling from my right eye. I brushed it away.

"Don't be sad. This is what I want."

I nodded.

Blinking rapidly, I rolled my shoulders back.

"If you're sure?" I checked once more.

She smiled brightly. "I am."

I asked the question. "Maggie, would you like to cross over? May I ask you to move on?"

"Yes," she replied.

I gave her a little magickal push. "Safe crossing," I whispered.

"Thank you." Her voice was the rustle of paper caught in a soft breeze and, just like that, she was gone.

CHAPTER TWENTY

"Did you leave Maggie behind?" Delilah popped her head out of the kitchen as soon as I made it back to Hedge Cottage. She had donned one of Millicent's homemade pinafore aprons, red and white gingham check with a zesty yellow feathered fringe around the chest area. Cheerful in a shouldn't-be-seen-dead-in-it kind of way.

Gertie looked up from the sofa expectantly. Marissa was sitting on the floor in front of her. I couldn't tell what they had been up to, but at least the dogs were still settled.

I gave a warning headshake. "Maggie had to go somewhere," I told them.

"Did she go home?" Gertie asked.

"Yes," I said, just about ready to dissolve into exhausted, emotional tears again, "she went home."

"She might have said goodbye," Gertie pouted,

but I could tell from the looks on the faces of the other women that they understood there was more to it than that.

"Hey!" I tried to sound cheerful. "Look what I found." I held up the slice of rose quartz so that it caught the light.

"You found it!" Marissa laughed in relief.

"I told you it was in the box," Gertie huffed.

"Well, you weren't wrong," I said. "It had dropped out, but I found it with Maggie's help."

"That's good," Gertie sniffed. "I'm bored. Can I turn on the TV?"

Marissa stroked her head. "No, darling. Millicent is sleeping."

"It won't wake her up!"

"All thanks to you, honey," Venus called from the kitchen.

"No, but we will," I said quickly. "Very soon." I joined Delilah and Venus—also wearing one of Millicent's aprons, this one in the shape of a giant purple rabbit's head—in the kitchen. "How are we doing?" I asked.

Delilah stirred the contents of the cauldron. The thick pink liquid simmered away over a flame. The scent of offal was slightly overwhelming. "Nearly there. Venus kindly dealt with the ox heart for me—"

"Oh, that was good of her." I shot Venus a look. She smirked at me.

"Yes. It saved me doing it," Delilah said. "I'm not very good with blood and flesh and things of that sort."

"I really don't know how a witch can be afraid of such things," Venus huffed. "There are far worse things."

"Like what?" I asked.

Venus nodded at the kitchen door. "Children."

"That's harsh," I said.

"Don't judge me," Venus said. "I'm standing here in a kitchen no bigger than a pigpen, wearing an apron and *cooking*—something I usually refuse point blank to do—in order to wake up an ex-boyfriend, in a part of the country that barely makes it onto the map of the British Isles, let alone Europe, and *all because of a child.*"

She had a point.

"So sue me," she finished.

Delilah giggled. "I have to confess I never wanted children either."

I glanced at the door. "I think I'm having second thoughts."

"Then we're in agreement!" Venus sounded

happy. "We should toast to that. I found some rhubarb wine in the pantry."

"We can't just drink the contents of Millicent's larder!" Delilah sounded appalled, but I had to confess, after the emotional turmoil of letting Maggie go, it seemed like a good to me.

"She won't mind," I said. "Let me find some glasses."

"The crystal?" Delilah reminded me.

"Oh yes." I uncurled my fingers. The crystal lay on the palm of my hand, looking oddly insignificant. "What do we do? Just chuck it in there?"

Venus perused the recipe once more. "Looks like it. Perhaps we should ask the child to recant the hex?"

"Good idea," Delilah agreed. "She should do it while she's stirring the mixture."

"Are you guys just making this up?" I asked.

"Pretty much," Venus said, and Delilah nodded agreement. "The recipe is vague."

We called Gertie through to the kitchen and she arrived with her entourage: Sampson, Sunny, Jasper and Marissa. I handed over the crystal carefully. "Gertie? We need you to recant the spell—"

"What does that mean?"

Marissa bent down to place an arm around her

niece's shoulders. "It means you have to take back what you asked for when you cast the spell in the first place. Can you do that?"

Gertie stuck her bottom lip out. "Will all this be over then?"

"Yes," said Venus.

"Will the lady cure my tummy ache?"

"She will," I promised.

"But …" Gertie's voice became very small, "the doggies will have to go home."

"Yes, they will," Marissa said. "But that's a good thing. Their owners will miss them otherwise."

Gertie sighed. "I'll miss them too."

"It's a good lesson to learn," Venus said. "Actions have consequences."

I hastily nudged Venus with my elbow. The last thing we needed right now was for Gertie to get upset and refuse to recant.

"Perhaps if we get it all sorted out today, you and Marissa could stay for Christmas and you might hear from Father Christmas?"

Gertie's face lit up. "Really?"

"You have nothing to lose by trying," I smiled. "Shall we have a go?" I asked Gertie.

She nodded with a little more enthusiasm. Delilah grabbed one of the kitchen chairs and brought it over in front of Millicent's stove. Marissa lifted Gertie onto the chair so that she could stir the contents of the cauldron.

"Hold out your hand," I said. She did so and I dropped the crystal into her palm. I stood back, motioning to the others to follow suit, allowing Gertie the time and space she needed. Spellcasting can be a personal business.

"I don't know how to do it," she whimpered.

"Say, 'With this stone, I invoke the power of the goddesses'," Marissa instructed her.

"And then just put it in your own words," Delilah added.

"It's the thought behind it that counts," I finished.

In the end, what she asked for was simple and to the point. Unaccustomed as she was to creating magick, she stumbled over language that did not come easily, but which she had evidently read in the spell book in the bookshop or overheard Marissa use. "With this stone, I invoke the power of the goddesses," she repeated, then took a deep breath. "I wanted a mummy and a daddy and a dog and a Christmas present and I wanted Silvan and Marissa to be together. I asked for Silvan to fall asleep and for Marissa to wake him up, but I didn't know it would be such big magick and cause bad things to happen."

"Take it back," whispered Marissa.

"So I take it back. Undo. Undo. Undo."

"The power of three makes it so," intoned Delilah.

I nodded at Gertie and she dropped the stone into the cauldron. The thick red mixture hissed and spat, rolled up the side of the cauldron and belched a cloud of raspberry-offal flavoured steam into the air before settling back down.

"So must it be," I said, and the others followed suit.

I lay a hand on Gertie's head. "There's nothing to do now but wait."

CHAPTER TWENTY-ONE

I raided Millicent's cupboards for some wine goblets and snacks. In a faded confectionery tin on the counter I found some of her freshly baked cheese scones, probably prepared in time for my Yule feast. I felt slightly bad about stealing them, but needs must, and I was sure she would understand.

Only Delilah, a vegan, declined the scone; everyone else accepted one with lashings of butter. We sat on the floor of the lounge—between them, Millicent, Gertie and the dogs took up all the available room on the sofa and none of us wanted to be the one that pinched the single armchair—and sipped at the rhubarb wine and nibbled the exquisitely flavoursome scones, while the cauldron bubbled and whistled most peculiarly, unwatched in the kitchen.

Eventually, Gertie dozed off and we whispered

together, part cackling coven, part harem of Silvan's loves. In due course, predictably, talk turned to Maggie.

"What happened?" Delilah wanted to know.

I blew my cheeks out. "She wanted to cross over."

"And you can do that?" Venus sounded sceptical.

"Yes. It's not something I like to do, but it is a gift. A blessing and a curse, perhaps."

"I'm surprised she didn't want to say goodbye." Delilah almost sounded like Gertie. A hurt child.

Marissa reached out and patted her knee. "Perhaps she thought it would be easier to just take the opportunity to go." She nodded at her niece. "It would have been difficult to do that in front of Gertie."

Delilah nodded. "That's true."

"She was looking forward to new adventures," I recalled.

"Let's hope she finds them." Venus raised her glass and we all quietly toasted Maggie's onward journey.

I leaned back against the wall, enjoying the wine, beginning to mellow out a little, thinking of Maggie and Silvan and imagining the experiences they had shared as young people just starting out on life. She had been right. Those were memories to treasure.

Delilah suddenly jolted upright, the wine sloshing in her goblet and splashing on her gingham apron. "I've just had a thought!"

"I don't like the sound of that," Venus groaned and rolled her eyes.

"Go on," I said.

"The recipe book said we have to strain the mixture through red silk," Delilah said.

Marissa looked around. "Does Millicent have any?"

I had no idea. "We'll have to have a scout around," I said, reluctantly levering myself up. "She does a lot of crafty stuff; she must have a material stash somewhere."

Marissa joined me in the search. We located reams of fat quarters and rolls of odds and ends of material, neatly folded away in a sideboard. Red cotton, red velvet, red wool and red felt but, unfortunately, no red silk.

I examined the throws and cushions—Millicent adored unusual fabrics, especially ones that clashed—but again, there was no silk.

"What about a blouse or something?" Venus suggested. "Would she have one in her wardrobe?"

I pulled a face. Would Millicent own anything as dull as a plain red silk blouse? "I suppose I could have a quick look in her room." I really didn't like the idea of that at all. It seemed a step too far.

"I'll come with you," Venus offered and, strength in numbers, we made our way upstairs, followed by a slightly indignant hairy lurcher.

"Sorry, Jasper," I said as I pushed open the door to the front bedroom. He trotted ahead of me and jumped on the bed, growling a little, as though to say I wasn't welcome in his mistress's inner sanctum.

In all the time I'd known Millicent, I had never visited the upstairs of Hedge Cottage. Her bedroom was a definite extension of her personality. Warm and clean and colourful. The bed was a double, with a carved wooden headboard, covered in a fat squidgy quilt and a gorgeous soft woollen throw of midnight blue with gold embellishments. Multi-coloured cushions had been tossed at the head of the bed, seemingly indiscriminately, and yet the overall effect was pretty in a bright, random way. I had the urge to lie down and sleep for a hundred years.

There wasn't a hope that Jasper would allow that.

The walls were different colours. A soft pastel lilac,

a warm peach, a light sky blue and a darker violet behind the bed. There were several pictures in frames and a pair of gilt-edged mirrors. On the bedside table was a large pile of books and some spectacles. The furniture was plain but good quality wood, and the rug an expensive-looking silk creation from somewhere far away.

I shot a hasty glance at Jasper, who glared at me in return, his impressively hairy eyebrows low over his eyes, before pulling open the wardrobe door. Millicent had curated an impressive clothing collection over the years ... and when I say impressive, I obviously mean, impressively awful. Why wear items that match when you can really go to town with something that jars the eye or turns the stomach? It was, therefore, a surprise to me to see that Millicent had ordered the contents of her wardrobe ... by colour.

I pulled open the second door so that Venus and I could gape in fascination. The clothes ran the whole gamut of the spectrum, and Millicent had managed to arrange the shades of each colour in sequence too, so that it was like gazing at a fifty-piece felt tip collection of the kind I had loved as a child. I'd always kept my pens in that perfect rainbow layout for as long as I could, before my favourite colours began to run out and the remainders were relegated to my pencil case.

And, like my pens, there was nothing in the wardrobe in white or beige. One had to applaud Millicent for that, at least.

"That's just so … organised!" Venus could hardly contain herself.

I ran my fingers along the sleeves closest to me. "I had this idea that Millicent simply threw her clothes on in the dark," I said. "I didn't realise that she consciously chose to wear what she does." I shuddered. "Come to think of it, that might make it worse, actually."

Venus was hardly listening. "I do love a well-organised wardrobe." She peered more closely at the red section. "Let's see …"

We methodically worked our way through the red clothes. Polyester. *Ick.* Cotton. Wool. Viscose. Velvet.

The only obvious silk items were blouses, one in black and one in forest green with mauve zebra stripes. I hadn't seen her wearing that one.

Thank goodness.

Venus stood back, shaking her head. "Nada. What about back at the inn? Do you have anything in red silk?"

"Me?" I blinked. "Hardly. Some of my t-shirts have a bit of colour in them, but even my underwear is uniformly black."

"Underwear," Venus mused. "That's a thought. You know, I'm wearing silk knickers."

I stepped away from her. "TMI!"

"They're not red," she carried on, "so you can't have them."

"I don't care!" I stuffed my fingers—ineffectually—in my ears.

Venus jerked her thumb towards Millicent's dresser. "Maybe Millicent has red silk underwear."

My face crumpled. "No! I don't want to look."

Venus gripped my arm. "Be brave, Alf. Do it for Silvan." We stared at each other for a moment before she cackled.

"You're thoroughly evil," I growled, secretly amused, and reluctantly pulled open Millicent's top drawer. And there, by some miracle, was a pair of red underpants. I hooked a finger into the material and yanked them free. They certainly felt like silk to my uninitiated touch.

Venus snatched them off me and shook them out, smiling gleefully. A huge pair of bright red bloomers, the sort of thing Gwyn might have worn once upon a time. "Definitely silk!" Venus announced.

Finally, we were in luck.

It took four of us to strain the liquid. Two to heft the heavy cauldron, one to hold a bowl steady underneath and one to hold the bloomers taut. I don't know if you've ever tried to strain liquid through silk, but it can be a slow and arduous process, particularly given that our liquid—thanks to the blended ox heart—was quite thick and lumpy.

The stench was something else too. I was acting as one of the cauldron bearers and found I had to turn my head away, otherwise I might have seen the unwelcome resurgence of my cheese scone and rhubarb wine.

Finally, after lots of moaning and groaning from all quarters, and a few choice curses from Venus, we had saved all the liquid we could manage. We were left with a clear raspberry-red concoction in the bowl, and a pair of ruined silk bloomers.

"What should I do with these?" Delilah had turned green.

"We could wash them?" Marissa sounded doubtful.

"Oh, goodness," sighed Delilah.

I too quivered at that thought. "Let's just chuck them out."

Marissa stayed Delilah with a wave of her hand. "What about the crystal? Do we need that again?"

"We might do." Venus waited for one of us to search through the meaty remnants pooled in the bloomers. When none of us made a move to do so, she tutted loudly and dived in herself. She extracted the sliver of crystal with a flourish.

Delilah, retching, wadded the bloomers up and went in search of the bin outside.

Venus set the crystal on the draining board and lifted the bowl. "How much do we have here? About two-thirds of a pint?"

Marissa handed her a potion bottle and we watched as Venus carefully decanted the mixture. The bottle wasn't close to full.

"It looks like it," I agreed. "Not a huge amount after all that effort. And how does it even work? How do we dispense it?"

We huddled around the recipe book again. There were no further written instructions. I flipped over to the next page. *A Spell to Straighten Curly Hair*.

"Hmm." I filed that one away for future reference and turned back to the *True Love's Kiss* page.

"How in the goddess's name are we supposed to know what to do?" My frustration threatened to boil over.

"I guess we could give a teaspoon to Millicent and see if she wakes up?" suggested Marissa.

I stepped into the lounge and stared at my friend, slumbering peacefully. Jasper had climbed back up and had tucked his head in her lap. Gertie lay on her side next to him, also sleeping, her hand on Sampson's flank as he napped next to her.

"I suppose so." I didn't like the idea of Millicent being the guinea pig, but what other option was there? Venus handed me the bottle and a teaspoon.

"How much?" I wondered aloud.

"Perhaps start with a quarter of a teaspoon and take it from there?" Delilah, always sensible, suggested.

I nodded and moved closer to Millicent. Jasper gave me a warning growl.

"It's alright," I told him. "I'm trying to wake Millie up."

He settled again, his ears flat against his neck.

I waved the bottle under Millicent's nose as though it contained smelling salts. Her eyelids flickered, which seemed like a good sign to me. I tipped the bottle and dripped some of the mixture onto the spoon, more like a half than a quarter. I hesitated then took the plunge, slipping the mixture into Millicent's mouth. Some of it dribbled out from the side and I hurriedly wiped the excess away with my fingers. Even in her sleep she was capable of swallowing, and she did so.

But she didn't wake up.

I poured another half a teaspoon and tried again, with exactly the same result. More dribbles. She swallowed, but her eyes didn't so much as twitch.

Now I had a quandary. I held the bottle poised above the spoon. How much was too much?

Suddenly my confidence evaporated away. I couldn't do it. Couldn't risk anything happening to Millicent. It wouldn't have been fair to use her a guinea pig just because I wanted to wake Silvan up.

I turned back to the women gathered at the kitchen door, their hair dishevelled, their aprons stained. Even Venus had gore smeared all over her face and hands. All of them appeared as tired as I felt. And behind them, Millicent's normally pristine kitchen looked like a slaughterhouse.

"I think we need to run any further experiments on Silvan," I said.

Chapter Twenty-Two

We abandoned poor Millicent where she snoozed and trudged back to the inn with the dogs walking behind us. This time even Gertie was too weary to complain about the distance and being moved from pillar to post.

Gwyn waited in reception, surrounded by dogs, all of whom were naturally ecstatic to see the rest of us. My grandmama's mouth was set in a sombre line, however. "You haven't managed …?" she asked above the din of several dozen dogs barking. The question hung in the air, and I lifted the bottle of potion to show her.

"We created this. It's the antidote to the Somnus hex. I gave some to Millicent but she didn't wake up. I don't suppose anything changed here?" I asked, ever hopeful.

"Absolutely nothing, Alfhild." Gwyn glared

around at her pack. "Will you hush!" she trilled, and for some reason they did.

"Grandmama's a Dog Whisperer," I said. *Who knew?*

She was right that nothing had changed, though, apart from maybe a few new additions to her canine fan club. I traipsed through the bar to the kitchen, casting a sorrowful eye over my sleeping guests and Zephaniah slumped behind the counter, while trying not to trip over those dogs who were splayed out on the floor gnawing on toys, bones and the goddess knew what else. At least they were alive and happy, because elsewhere, everything was still and silent, just as we'd left it. Only in the kitchen was there anything approaching normality. The meats still roasted without burning and the vegetables steamed without becoming mush. Monsieur Emietter's moustache rippled as he snored.

"Help yourselves to more broth," I told the others as I rummaged in a drawer for a teaspoon.

Delilah jumped at the chance, but Venus patted her belly, evidently still full after Millicent's cheese scone. I envied her the capacity to eat one cheese scone and feel satisfied. I could have eaten a dozen and probably still have room for more.

"What about you, Gertie?" Marissa asked. "Would you like some soup?"

Gertie shook her head, her face a sullen mask. "Is Silvan going to wake up now?" she asked.

"I hope so," I said.

"Will the doggies go home?"

"I should think so." Certainly, if Gwyn had anything to do with it.

"Will Silvan play with me?"

I smiled at her. "I don't see why not."

She sniffed and slid onto the bench.

"Is your tummy still hurting?" Marissa asked her.

"A bit," Gertie replied. "The lady didn't wake up. Does that mean we can't undo my magick?"

"I'm sure we can undo it." I certainly hoped so. It wasn't too late to get the big wizarding guns in. Shadowmender and Mr Kephisto. "One way or another, we will sort everything out."

I waved the teaspoon at the others and headed for the door to the back passage.

"Alf!" Venus called. I turned back and she handed me the crystal. "I don't know if you need this, but you'd better take it just in case."

I nodded my thanks, stuck it in my pocket and slowly made my way upstairs.

The huge Irish wolfhound clambered laboriously to his feet as I walked onto the landing.

"Hey!" I greeted him. "Good job, fella. You can come and join my security detail any time you like." He licked my hand, obviously pleased with the job offer. I pushed open the office door. Charity was in exactly the same position she'd been in for the past ... thirty thousand years, or however long it had been.

"There'll be some cricked necks in this inn when they all wake up," I murmured and, leaving the door open, went next door to my bedroom, the Wolfhound resuming his sentry duty outside.

I stared down at my love, and then at Mr Hoo.

"Well, I'm back," I told them. "Did you miss me?"

Neither of them moved, but I figured they might be able to hear what was going on, like some coma patients can. It couldn't hurt to converse with Silvan. Don't doctors always say that?

"We found a recipe for the antidote," I told him, "and we created it to the best of our ability, but"—I perched next to him on the bed, my weight jiggling him—"unfortunately it didn't seem to work that well for Millicent." I held up the bottle. The dark pink liquid caught the limited light and shimmered. "I'm hoping that because the spell was initially aimed at you, if I give you this, it will wake the whole village up." I sighed. "A girl can dream, can't she?"

Except it wasn't me that was dreaming. It was him. And Mr Hoo. And Charity. And Millicent. And Stan and Rhona and the postmaster and the rest of the village.

This time I remembered to have a tissue ready. I un-stoppered the bottle, poured the potion onto the teaspoon and edged it between his lips. As with Millicent, some was swallowed, and some dribbled out. I mopped up the spillage, held my breath and waited.

Nothing.

I closed my eyes, uttered a little prayer and gave him another teaspoon.

And a third.

When he didn't respond at all, I placed the bottle on the bedside table and massaged my temples. What if he needed the whole bottle? What if we'd only created enough potion for one person? The rate I was getting through it, there wouldn't be any left for anyone else. I mean, of course we could make more potion. In fact, we had the space in Whittle Inn's kitchen to create industrial-scale quantities of it. But it did mean an awful lot more work and, downstairs, my potion posse were all exhausted.

"I don't know what to do," I whispered into the quiet room.

"When did that ever stop you before?" Gwyn apparated by my side, startling me.

I slouched onto the bed. "It would have been far easier if the potion recipe book had given us more detailed instructions for using the antidote and casting a recant spell," I said.

"Magick is not supposed to be easy, Alfhild. If it were, then any old mundane Tom, Dick and Harriet would think they were witches."

"And we can't have that." I arched an eyebrow.

"No, indeed."

"Do you have any suggestions?" I asked.

"I have plenty, but not all of them are pertinent to the situation in hand."

I rolled my eyes. She could be so waspish. "Any advice then, Grandmama? I'd be happy to hear constructive suggestions."

Gwyn folded her arms and levelled me with a hard stare. "Why don't *you* take the potion, my dear?"

"Me?" I curled a lip. That was the daftest thing I'd ever heard. "I'm not asleep."

"Well, exactly. Has it never occurred to you *why* you're not asleep? Why *you*, of all people, were spared?"

It had, of course, but I'd never come up with a satisfactory answer.

I frowned. She had a point.

"Consider this. We'll never know exactly what Gertie said, although her intentions were clear. It is therefore exceedingly difficult to undo the spell." Gwyn paused, thinking for a moment. "It strikes me, however, that in her mind, she was creating a get-out clause that would wake Silvan up."

"She wanted Marissa to be the hero of the moment."

Gwyn nodded. "And she was drawn to the Somnus Hex and the notion of Silvan being woken up by his true love."

"It's the potion that's the true love, rather than a person," I pointed out. "True Love's Kiss is just its name."

"Not without reason, surely?" Gwyn tutted. "Think, Alfhild. In magick, intention is everything. Gertie wanted Silvan to be woken by his true love. In reality, she knows that Marissa and Silvan are only friends because Marissa has told her so. In her heart of hearts, she knows that Silvan has a true-life partner."

"She did know about me," I agreed. "And so, when she cast the spell, while she *wanted* Marissa and Silvan to be together, the person she *envisaged* waking him up ... was me? That's what you're suggesting?"

"That's precisely what I'm suggesting. But also, by opening the box, *you* were the one who let the spell loose. All of this revolves around you."

That made sense.

"Always in trouble," Gwyn said and apparated away.

I opened my mouth to offer a tart response and then closed it again. What would be the point? She was right.

I eyed the potion with distaste. Did I really have to drink it? How much? And what about the crystal?

I sniffed the bottle. The faint tang of raspberry and cherry mingled with a less pleasant earthy smell.

"By all that's green!" I held it to my mouth. Licked my lips. Took a deep breath.

And chickened out.

"It's not going to kill me, is it?" I chided myself and replaced it on the bedside table. "I've done worse things than drink blended ox heart."

I felt inside my pocket for the crystal and drew it out. Such a sad chip of pink rose quartz. And yet so immensely powerful. Look at what it had achieved. I held it between my finger and thumb and stared at it in the lamplight. It had a slight flaw.

That raised it in my estimation.

I palmed the stone and lifted the bottle once more.

"Faint heart never won dark gentleman," I grumbled, and drank the liquid down in one.

A warm raspberry scented breeze wafted over me and, suddenly exhausted, I closed my eyes and sank against the pillows.

CHAPTER TWENTY-THREE

"Hooo-oooo!"

"Are you tired?" Silvan's voice reached me as though from a great distance.

"Wha—?" I blinked and jerked upright, nearly headbutting him in the process. Not far away at all. Right here with me, in fact. Behind him, Mr Hoo's head wobbled.

"Hoooooooooo?"

"Yes, I'm awake," I told my owl. My brain seemed full of cotton wool.

"You were snoring," Silvan said.

"I don't snore. What time is it?" I frowned, trying to get my bearings. Outside the bedroom door I could hear the sound of a vacuum cleaner. What had happened? "You're awake?" I asked him.

"It's nice to see you too, Alfie." Silvan cocked his head at me, his dark eyes glinting with amusement.

"You've been back for days," I mumbled, shaking my head and trying to get rid of the fuddled heavy feeling inside.

"I beg to differ." Silvan pointed at the bedside clock. Three fifty-nine. *How was that even possible?*

"You've been asleep for … for … forever!" I said.

"Just a quick nap while I was waiting for *you*."

The vacuum cleaner stopped its howling, which brought me some relief. "I really don't like these new-fangled machines," I heard Florence say. "The hose and the wires get so tangled …" Her voice faded away, only to be replaced by the jangle of a tambourine or something similar and the squawk of a crumhorn.

"Don't you be playing that down this corridor, Luppitt Smeatharpe!" Florence barked. "Miss Charity is trying to work. And the Lord alone knows what Miss Alf is doing."

"Beg your pardon, Miss Florence," said Luppitt. "We have to get some practice in for the party."

"That's as maybe, but not up here you don't! Go and set up in Speckled Wood!"

"But it's started to snow," Luppitt protested.

"Away with you," scolded Florence. I heard the clunk of the vacuum as she pulled it past my door. "And that reminds me, I'd better check on Monsieur

Emietter." Her voice drifted away. Downstairs, the grandfather clock was chiming.

Bong. Bong. Bong. Bong.

Four o'clock!

The wall behind my head vibrated as the Bakelite phone on the desk in the office began to ring. I distinctly heard Charity's dulcet tones sing out, "Whittle Inn, Charity speaking. How may I help you today?"

"Oh, thank the goddesses," I whispered.

Silvan sank onto the bed beside me, his eyes questioning. "I've had some very strange dreams."

"Hooo-ooo-oooo!" Mr Hoo agreed.

"Have you?"

"Mmm. People from my past." Something wistful crossed his face, the briefest of shadows, quickly replaced by concern for me. "Do you want to tell me what's going on?"

"It's a rather long story," I said, cupping his cheek with one hand. "And some of it might be difficult for you to hear."

"Alf?" From somewhere down the corridor I heard a woman calling my name. "Alfhild?"

"Yes?" I called back. That seemed to be a signal for the Irish wolfhound to start barking. His deep woof provided a stimulus that set the others off, like some kind of round robin for dogs. In seconds, every dog in every corner of the inn, on every cushion and sofa and bed, had taken up the call.

Mr Hoo leapt from the bed and flew to the window, where he landed on the settle and regarded me with a certain distrust that suggested he suspected I'd betrayed him by allowing a pack of ferocious wolves into his inn.

Silvan, too, jumped to his feet and reached for his wand.

"Wait!" I called. "It's alright!" But he'd thrown open the door and whirled into the corridor.

"What is that racket?" Charity shouted from next door. "I'm on the phone!"

"Hoo! Hoo! Hoo!"

"Where have all these dogs come from?" Silvan asked.

"Hoooo-ooo!"

I shot a reassuring glance at Mr Hoo, slipped off the bed and dashed to the door after Silvan. I was just in time to see him spot the woman walking up the corridor. He did a double take, but she addressed me instead.

"Alf? Isn't it wonderful? We've done it! Everything's back to normal!"

Silvan took an involuntary step backwards,

standing on my foot. "Delilah?" he asked in disbelief. "What are you doing here?"

I hopped up and down in agony, certain he'd crushed my metatarsal or something and I'd never walk properly again.

"Silvan? You're awake!" She laughed and hurled her arms around him. "At last!"

He hugged Delilah, but his face turned to me. *What on earth is going on?* he seemed to be asking. "At last?" he repeated. "What do you mean?"

"You don't know the half of it," I told him.

CHAPTER TWENTY-FOUR

"I'm sorry." Gertie snuggled against Silvan, one arm wrapped around Sampson on the other side of her. "I did bad magick."

We had gathered in The Snug, away from Monsieur Emietter and his meat cleaver in the kitchen. For some reason, my chef thought he was behind schedule with tonight's feast—believe it or not, it turned out it was still the twenty-first of December—and he was spitting feathers because all of his vegetable broth had mysteriously disappeared and he'd have to make more.

"You did make bad magick," Silvan agreed. "Do you realise how much stress you caused for your poor Aunt Marissa?"

"Yes," Gertie nodded, her eyes huge as she stared up at Silvan's tanned face.

"Not to mention poor old Alfie. Without her and

Delilah and Venus, there might not have been a future for any of us." Silvan looked suitably sombre.

"And Maggie," Gertie said. Silvan winced. I'd explained everything to him, without going into too much detail. There would be time for that. But I knew Maggie was something he would need to get his head around.

"You have to promise me not to do any more magick unless you're at school and under proper tuition, okay?"

"Okay."

"If I were you, I'd suggest she doesn't do any magick until she goes to university, myself," Venus chipped in. I was inclined to agree.

Silvan concentrated on Gertie. "Swear on your—"

Marissa made a small noise in her throat.

Silvan backed down hurriedly. "Alright, no swearing on anything."

I sniggered.

Charity's mobile began to ring. She glanced at the display. "Millicent," she said. "She probably wants to talk about tonight's plans."

Delilah, Venus and I exchanged glances. *Uh-oh*.

"Hi, Mills," sang Charity. Even above the general hubbub in the room—the people, the dogs, the ghosts—I could hear Millicent's indignant tones.

Charity, slightly taken aback, removed the phone from her ear. "Alf? Millicent has been trying to call you."

I'd left my phone upstairs. Accidentally on purpose. "Has she?" I asked in faux surprise and began to back away to the door.

"She wants to know why her kitchen looks like a whole battalion of wizards has been murdered in there?"

"Er ... right." I looked to kind-hearted Delilah for support. She avoided my gaze.

"What should I say?" Charity asked.

"Why does she assume I had anything to do with it?"

"Are you kidding?" Charity said, without even consulting Millicent. "If there's something dodgy going down in Whittlecombe, *of course* you're behind it."

"Oh, so that's the way it is, is it?" I grumbled, working hurt indignance.

Silvan laughed. "Your reputation precedes you, Alfie."

"She also wants to know what you've done with her dogs," Charity nodded meaningfully at Jasper and Sunny. The Yorkshire terrier was lying in front of the fireplace, completely at home, but Jasper was sitting up, his fluffy ears alert, listening to his mistress giving Charity an earful. He gave me his evil eye and barked once, twice, loudly. I heard Millicent's voice rise in response.

Charity removed the phone from her ear once more and lay it against her chest. "She wants her dogs back. As soon as. Please." She quirked an eyebrow. "I'm paraphrasing. She's mad enough to consider turning you into a bat."

The cheek!

"Alright! Okay!" I held my hands up in surrender. "No rest for the—" No. It was probably best not to admit to being wicked. "Tell her I'm on my way. We need to get all of the dogs back to their rightful owners anyhow. People will think there's been a dognapper in town."

Charity relayed the message to Millicent and hung up. She wafted a hand as though she were hot. "She's not happy."

Gertie's face crumpled. "I don't want the doggies to go home!" Sampson stood up and began to lick her face. "I love the doggies."

Silvan took her chin gently in his hand. "But if you were to keep them, that would be stealing,

Gertie. These dogs belong to people who love them very much."

"I know, but—"

"No buts," Silvan said firmly. "You need to learn that if you do something wrong, you have to make amends. You have to put things right. That's the way the world works best. As a witch, you will see that everything must be held in balance. *You* cast a spell and that spell had to be undone. Now *you* have to make sure that all these dogs get home safely."

"You're coming with me?" I asked hopefully.

"Of course," said Silvan. "Aren't we, Gertie?"

Outside was now full dark, and the sleet of earlier had, as Luppitt had told Florence, finally turned to snow. The ground was very wet so I wasn't sure the snow would stick, but anything was a possibility once the temperature dropped below zero.

We strolled down into Whittlecombe with forty-seven dogs in tow. I know the number because Gertie counted each and every one. I felt like the Pied Piper of Hamelin, no word of a lie. None of our canine friends needed leads, which was just as well because I only had two, one for Sunny and one for

Jasper. The rest of the dogs simply followed us calmly down the centre of the road. The going was slow, as you might imagine. Occasionally one would scamper off to sniff the bushes, and passing a lamp-post was a nightmare because one after another they had to sniff and tiddle, but eventually we reached Hedge Cottage.

I almost felt afraid to knock, for fear of how angry she might be, but as Silvan had so recently said, it's important to make the wrongs right. I braced myself and tapped on the door. Normally I would have knocked and entered, but I felt like I'd done enough trespassing for one day.

Millicent threw open the door and stared at me expectantly, her face giving nothing away. Beside me, Sunny and Jasper stood quietly and waited, as though they knew I needed to make my own penance.

"I'm really sorry," I said. "I can come and clean up for you after I've returned all these dogs to their rightful homes."

Millicent edged her head through the doorway, out into the snow. Flakes settled on her hair as she stared in surprise at Silvan and Gertie and their forty-five furry companions.

"Hi, Millie!" Silvan beamed at her.

"Hello, Mrs Ballicott. Sorry about taking your dogs away," called Gertie.

Millicent waved at them and narrowed her eyes at me. "What have you been up to?"

"Well—" I took a deep breath.

She held up one hand. "Save it. You can tell me all about it later. Around the bonfire with a bottle of rhubarb wine."

I breathed a sigh of relief. "So we're still friends, then?"

"Of course we are, you big silly." She reached for me and gave me a hug. "But about the cleaning—"

"I can come back," I promised.

"No, that's quite alright, Alf. I doubt you can clean to my standards."

"I—"

"No," she replied firmly. "I'll use magick. Or you can lend me Florence if she's amenable."

"Always," I said.

"Thank goodness for her!"

Finding the right home for each dog was much easier than you might have supposed. Some of them had their addresses on their collar tags, others had a phone number, and even those who had neither knew where they lived. They would dart off from the pack as we approached a gate or boundary and disappear through a hole in the hedge or bound over the fence.

The pair of border collies darted off up a lane towards a farm, the whippet slid between the gateposts of a rather grand detached house near the church and the Irish wolfhound simply sat on the front step of a tiny cottage behind the village pond and barked several times. His deep woof brought his owner running to the door.

"Mouse?" the old man asked. "Where have you been? How did you get out?"

Mouse? I had a little giggle at that.

In just under an hour, we had parted company with all bar one.

Sampson.

Gertie and I knelt next to him. He was wearing a collar but it had no tag. "Can you hold him while I have a look at his collar?" I asked her, and she did so, firmly but gently. I removed it. It was an old blue cotton one, faded and dirty. Sometimes people like to sew their details on the reverse of the collar, but this one yielded no clues.

I slipped it back around Sampson's neck and shrugged. "Nothing."

Silvan pointed at Whittle Stores. The post office and café were in darkness now, closed for the evening, but Stan and Rhona stayed open until eight most nights. "Let's ask in there."

Silvan and Gertie waited outside while I went in.

"Hi, Alf!" Rhona greeted me. "What can I get for you this evening?"

I glanced around, noting a couple of stray mushrooms on the floor. "Hi, Rhona," I smiled. "I have a query about a dog."

"A dog?"

I pointed at Gertie and Silvan waiting outside. "We found this little dog. He's been up at the inn with us for a … erm … a little while. I want to try and locate his owner."

"Is he a stray?" Rhona came to the door with me. "I don't recognise him. I think I know most of the dogs that live in the village."

"How strange," I said.

"I tell you what, we can put a card in the window if you like. Everyone reads the Lost and Found when they're hanging around outside. You may get lucky. Someone will know who he belongs to."

"Good idea." She slid a plain postcard over the counter and I quickly filled it in with his details.

"That'll be fifty pence, please."

I had to pay for it? *Sheesh*. You know what they say, no good deed goes unpunished. "Rightio." I fumbled around to find my purse. "I'd better have some dog food if he's coming back to the inn with me." Gertie would be pleased.

"You know, that's a funny thing." Rhona dug around on the bottom shelf, reaching into the far recesses. "We've sold so much dog food today. I haven't seen the going of it."

"Really?" I said, trying not to laugh.

"Yes. It's all accounted for in the takings, but strange nonetheless."

"Very odd." I handed over a pound and waited for the change. "Will I see you later?" I asked.

"At your bonfire? We wouldn't miss it for the world."

EPILOGUE

In the clearing in Speckled Wood, the bonfire crackled and hissed as Ned and Finbarr fed the flames. Embers flew upwards, while flurries of snow circled down, the air a riot of red and white. Very Christmassy.

I'd chosen to sit on the bench furthest away from where Luppitt and the rest of the Devonshire Fellows were squawking out their version of *Fairytale of New York* but, secretly, I had to admire their skill at playing their instruments and the way in which they could take a modern classic and murder it in their own inimitable Elizabethan style.

I accepted another cup of mulled cider from Venus and we huddled together on the bench with Delilah, just a little too far from the fire to keep warm. We could have danced, that would have warmed us up, but we were all exhausted.

"I love Yule," I told them, "but tonight, I just don't have the energy."

"Same." Venus swigged at the cider and lifted her cup. "This is very nice, but it will send me to sleep if I'm not careful."

"I'm thinking of crawling under a bush," Delilah agreed. "Not even this amazing music would keep me awake. You're so lucky to have such a talented troupe of musicians living with you, Alf."

"Indeed." I tried, in the spirit of the season, not to sound too unenthusiastic. I changed the subject instead. "Wizard Shadowmender has suggested that when we wake up in the morning, time will have righted itself and we will lose the intervening days."

"So tomorrow will be—" Delilah screwed her face up, trying to work it out.

"Christmas Eve."

"Time flies—" Venus said.

"—when you're having fun," the three of us finished together. We laughed and clinked cups.

"What plans did you two have for tonight?" I asked.

"Before you rudely dragged us away from our lives?" Venus asked.

I awaited her disapproval, imagining she'd had some celebrity event to attend somewhere, but she only shrugged. "Some vampire ball in Westminster. I'm glad to have missed it, to be honest. Vampires bore me so."

Delilah gaped at her. "You party with vampires? I've never met a single one."

"You're lucky," I said, with feeling. "They are the spawn of the devil."

Venus and I clinked cups again. "I'll drink to that, sister!"

"I thought you'd reserved that title for Gertie, Venus?" Delilah smiled.

"Ha!" As Venus nodded in the direction of the space that had been cleared for dancing, I followed her gaze. Gertie was twirling for Silvan and Marissa. "She's not so bad. Maybe."

"She'll be a powerful witch one day," I remarked. "Hopefully, Marissa will keep a close eye on her and keep her out of trouble. Imagine ... if she can do all that damage at her age without even knowing what she was doing ..."

"Total chaos. I sure am glad she's nothing to do with me," Venus said.

The music changed. *Frosty the Snowman*. Delilah jumped to her feet. "Oh, I love this one!" Without further ado, she rushed towards Silvan and grabbed his hand, forcing him to dance with her.

Venus and I giggled together.

"You don't mind?" Venus asked, nodding at the pair of them, Marissa joining them, although with less gay abandon than Delilah.

"Not at all," I said. "I like to see everyone having fun."

"You don't feel jealous at all when Silvan is with someone else?"

"Only Maysoon," I joked, but of course Venus didn't understand the reference. "No," I added. "I trust him."

"You are certainly well matched. Perhaps that's why you are his true love," Venus mused.

I certainly hoped I was.

"Do you intend to leave tomorrow?" I asked.

Venus raised her eyebrows. "Are you trying to get rid of me, Alfhild?"

"Absolutely not! It's been great getting to know you. I'm more than happy for you to stay here at the inn as my guest over Christmas, if you like?"

"Really?" Venus's face shone.

"Marissa and Gertie are staying. Delilah too. It will be a bit cramped but er ... Silvan and I can always sleep in the attic. I've done it before. That's if you don't have another swanky ball to go to, of course."

"I do," Venus said, her tone casual, "but I rather think I'd prefer to stay here for a few days with you guys."

"Smashing," I said. "It's settled then."

"Hey!" Silvan jigged his way over, his face pink with the combined exertion of dancing and a few tots of whisky, no doubt. He reached for my hand. "Come and dance with me."

I groaned. "No. I'm done in. I'm happy to sit here and watch."

He smiled down at me. "Spoilsport."

"You know it," I grinned back at him. "Venus will, though."

"Will I?" Venus asked in horror. "In these shoes?"

Venus was the only person I knew who would possibly think it was sensible to wear her stilettos in the woods. "I'd suggest taking them off," I said, "but it's pretty cold—"

The words were hardly out of my mouth before Venus leaned over and yanked the straps free of her feet. She kicked off her shoes. "Whatever, right? We only live once."

I laughed and clapped my hands. Silvan pulled Venus over to the other dancers. She was a neat mover, not as flamboyant as Delilah but not as reserved as Marissa.

"Are you having fun, my dear?" Gwyn floated next to me, dressed in an ice queen outfit I'd never seen her wearing before. White wool with a fur-lined trim. I hoped it was faux fur.

Mr Hoo flew down from the canopy above us and settled on a branch above her head. I smiled at him.

"Hooo-ooo!"

"I am, Grandmama. In spite of how hectic the last few days have been."

"You seem to have made a few new friends." She sounded like she approved.

"I honestly think I have." I'd never had many girlfriends of my own age before, but now I had a feeling that Marissa, Delilah, Venus and I, after our shared excursions, and in spite of our differences, would always have a strong friendship.

"That's something to be treasured," Gwyn said, indicating her own friends who were partying with us, members of Kappa Sigma Granma. "And of course you have your beau."

"At least for now." If the past few days had taught me anything, it was how fleeting some relationships could be.

"If I were to gaze into my crystal ball, I'm fairly certain the future would look bright for the two of you," Gwyn replied.

I narrowed my eyes. "Have you been scrying?" I asked.

"Perhaps." She pressed her lips together and turned her attention to the dancers. I knew what that look on her face meant. She wouldn't discuss it further. Some things should not be known.

Nonetheless, it was worth a try. "What else did your crystal ball tell you?"

Gwyn smirked. "Millicent has knitted Silvan a particularly hideous jumper for Christmas."

I grimaced, then checked Millicent couldn't see or hear us. She and Florence were engaged in a rather earnest conversation. I had a feeling Millicent wanted to know how to get ox-blood stains off her counter surfaces.

"Anything else?"

"It will be a lovely Christmas for our Charity. Minnie Frampton has sent the sparkling red shoes that she promised, the ones she wore to the Golden Wands earlier this year. They will fit beautifully. In addition, to add the proverbial icing to Charity's cake, Mike the Manchester Man will turn up here at eleven forty-two tomorrow—"

"And?"

"A certain little dog, found wandering homeless in Whittlecombe, will find his forever home with a penitent little girl, thanks to Father Christmas."

I smiled up at Gwyn. "That sounds perfect."

"I agree." Gwyn nodded in Silvan's direction. "So why don't you cast off your fatigue and dance with your young man?"

I watched him cavorting with the others, my heart warm with love for him. I'd do anything to ensure his happiness and wellbeing. "I should do," I said.

"Yes, you should. Yule and Christmas come but once a year, and you are only young for a short amount of time. Grab your joy with both hands."

The Devonshire Fellows had launched into *A Wombling Merry Christmas*. It just happened to be one of my most favourite ever Christmas tracks.

I stood and turned to face my great-grandmother. "I will. Thanks for all your support, Grandmama. You're the best."

She gave me a haughty look. "Really, Alfhild. No need to get mushy. That's what I'm here for."

I began to skirt the bonfire, making my way through the jigging revellers, intent on joining Silvan and the others, but something gave me pause. I glanced back towards the bench. For a second, I thought I saw Gwyn surrounded by dogs—dozens of ghost dogs of all shapes and sizes and varieties and flavours, her companions in the afterlife—but perhaps it was only a figment of my imagination. I blinked and they'd gone. She remained in place, alone, smiling after me.

"Merry Christmas, Grandmama," I said quietly. She would never have heard me above the hullaballoo, and although her lips didn't move, I clearly heard her response.

"Merry Christmas, my darling."

Need More Wonky?

Have you enjoyed *O' Witchy Town of Whittlecombe?*

Look out for more Wonky Inn stories in 2021.

If you enjoyed *O' Witchy Town of Whittlecombe* and you'd like to see even more *Wonky Inn*, please leave me a review on Amazon or Goodreads.

Reviews help spread the word about my work, which is great for me because I find new readers!

And why not join my mailing list to find out more about what I'm up to and what is coming out next?

If you'd like to join my closed author group you'll find it here at

NEED MORE WONKY?

www.facebook.com/
groups/JeannieWycherleysFiends

just let me know you've reviewed one of my books when you apply.

Playlist

If you'd like to listen to some of the music mentioned in this story, I've created a Spotify playlist called *O' Witchy Town of Whittlecombe*.

The link can be found right here

Or search for me on Spotify.

OUT NOW

The Creature from the Grim Mire

There's no chance of a quiet life when you've aliens in your attic.

Felicity Westmacott craves solitude.

But something with a hearty appetite is stalking the moor and terrifying the locals.

And things going bump in the night puts paid to her equilibrium.

As does the mysterious appearance of an elderly gentleman.
He claims to be a time traveller.

Obviously as nutty as a fruitcake, he wants her to run a creche.

For baby aliens.

Now her secret's out and other people are interested in Felicity's unusual house guests.

Her 'children' are in terrible danger.

Will Felicity save her young charges? Or will she finish her novel instead?

Find out in *The Creature from the Grim Mire*.

If you've ever wondered what HG Wells got up to in his spare time, you'll love this alien invasion tale set on Dartmoor in South Devon, UK. This is the perfect light-hearted read for lovers of humorous sci-fi mysteries or cozy animal mysteries, or indeed anyone seeking a bit of fun escapism with a cup of tea and a slice of cake.

But keep an eye on your snacks – there are hungry

aliens loose. Some of them can eat their body weight in Custard Creams!

The Creature from the Grim Mire is a collaboration between father and daughter, Peter Alderson Sharp (*The Sword, the Wolf and the Rock*) and Jeannie Wycherley (the Wonky Inn books, *Crone*, *The Municipality of Lost Souls* etc.).

The Complete Wonky Inn Series

The Wonkiest Witch: Wonky Inn Book 1

The Ghosts of Wonky Inn: Wonky Inn Book 2

Weird Wedding at Wonky Inn: Wonky Inn Book 3

The Witch Who Killed Christmas: Wonky Inn Christmas Special

<u>Fearful Fortunes and Terrible Tarot: Wonky Inn Book 4</u>

The Mystery of the Marsh Malaise: Wonky Inn Book 5

The Mysterious Mr Wylie: Wonky Inn Book 6

The Great Witchy Cake Off: Wonky Inn Book 7

Vengeful Vampire at Wonky Inn: Wonky Inn Book 8

Witching in a Winter Wonkyland: A Wonky Inn Christmas Cozy Special

<u>A Gaggle of Ghastly Grandmamas: Wonky Inn Book 9</u>

Magic, Murder and a Movie Star: Wonky Inn Book 10

O' Witchy Town of Whittlecombe: A Wonky Inn Christmas Cozy Special

Spellbound Hound

Ain't Nothing but a Pound Dog: Spellbound Hound Magic and Mystery Book 1

A Curse, a Coven and a Canine: Spellbound Hound Magic

and Mystery Book 2

Bark Side of the Moon: Spellbound Hound Magic and Mystery Book 3

Master of Puppies: Spellbound Hound Magic and Mystery Book 4 (TBC)

Midnight Garden: The Extra Ordinary World Novella Series Book 1

Beyond the Veil

Crone

A Concerto for the Dead and Dying

Deadly Encounters: A collection of short stories

Keepers of the Flame: A love story

Non-Fiction

Losing my best Friend: Thoughtful support for those affected by dog bereavement or pet loss

---

Follow Jeannie Wycherley

Find out more at on the website www.jeanniewycherley.co.uk

You can tweet Jeannie

twitter.com/Thecushionlady

Or visit her on Facebook for her fiction www.facebook.com/jeanniewycherley

Sign up for Jeannie's newsletter

eepurl.com/cN3Q6L